A CASE OF VIRGA

Volume 4: Zen and the Art of Investigation

ANTHONY WOLFF

authorHOUSE®

AuthorHouse™ LLC
1663 Liberty Drive
Bloomington, IN 47403
www.authorhouse.com
Phone: 1-800-839-8640

This is a work of fiction. All of the characters, names, incidents, organizations, and dialogue
in this novel are either the products of the author's imagination or are used fictitiously.

Published by AuthorHouse 3/11/2014

ISBN: 978-1-4918-6776-1 (sc)
ISBN: 978-1-4918-6824-9 (e)

PREFACE

WHO ARE THESE DETECTIVES ANYWAY?

"The eye cannot see itself" an old Zen adage informs us. The Private I's in these case files count on the truth of that statement. People may be self-concerned, but they are rarely self-aware.

In courts of law, guilt or innocence often depends upon its presentation. Juries do not - indeed, they may not - investigate any evidence in order to test its veracity. No, they are obliged to evaluate only what they are shown. Private Investigators, on the other hand, are obliged to look beneath surfaces and to prove to their satisfaction - not the court's - whether or not what appears to be true is actually true. The Private I must have a penetrating eye.

Intuition is a spiritual gift and this, no doubt, is why *Wagner & Tilson, Private Investigators* does its work so well.

At first glance the little group of P.I.s who solve these often baffling cases seem different from what we (having become familiar with video Dicks) consider "sleuths." They have no oddball sidekicks. They are not alcoholics. They get along well with cops.

George Wagner is the only one who was trained for the job. He obtained a degree in criminology from Temple University in Philadelphia and did exemplary work as an investigator with the Philadelphia Police. These were his golden years. He skied; he danced; he played tennis; he had a Porsche, a Labrador retriever, and a small sailboat. He got married and had a wife, two toddlers, and a house. He was handsome and well built, and he had great hair.

And then one night, in 1999, he and his partner walked into an ambush. His partner was killed and George was shot in the left knee and in his right shoulder's brachial plexus. The pain resulting from his injuries and the twenty-two surgeries he endured throughout the year that followed, left him addicted to a nearly constant morphine drip. By the time he was admitted to a rehab center in Southern California for treatment of his morphine addiction and for physical therapy, he had lost everything previously mentioned except his house, his handsome face, and his great hair.

His wife, tired of visiting a semi-conscious man, divorced him and married a man who had more than enough money to make child support payments unnecessary and, since he was the jealous type, undesirable. They moved far away, and despite the calls George placed and the money and gifts he sent, they soon tended to regard him as non-existent. His wife did have an orchid collection which she boarded with a plant nursery, paying for the plants' care until he was able to accept them. He gave his brother his car, his tennis racquets, his skis, and his sailboat.

At the age of thirty-four he was officially disabled, his right arm and hand had begun to wither slightly from limited use, a frequent result of a severe injury to that nerve center. His knee, too, was troublesome. He could not hold it in a bent position for an extended period of time; and when the weather was bad or he had been standing for too long, he limped a little.

George gave considerable thought to the "disease" of romantic love and decided that he had acquired an immunity to it. He would never again be vulnerable to its delirium. He did not realize that the gods of love regard such pronouncements as hubris of the worst kind and, as such, never allow it to go unpunished. George learned this lesson while working on the case, *The Monja Blanca*. A sweet girl, half his age and nearly half his weight, would fell him, as he put it, "as young David slew the big dumb Goliath." He understood that while he had no future with her, his future would be filled with her for as long as he had a mind that could think. She had been the victim of the most vicious swindlers he had ever encountered. They had successfully fled the country, but not the range of George's determination to apprehend them. These were master criminals, four of them, and he secretly vowed that he would make them fall, one by one. This was a serious quest. There was nothing quixotic about George Roberts Wagner.

While he was in the hospital receiving treatment for those fateful gunshot wounds, he met Beryl Tilson.

Beryl, a widow whose son Jack was then eleven years old, was working her way through college as a nurse's aid when she tended George. She had met him previously when he delivered a lecture on the curious differences between aggravated assault and attempted murder, a not uninteresting topic. During the year she tended him, they became friendly enough for him to communicate with her during the year he was in rehab. When he returned to Philadelphia, she picked him up at the airport, drove him home - to a house he had not been inside for two years - and helped him to get settled into a routine with the house and the botanical spoils of his divorce.

After receiving her degree in the Liberal Arts, Beryl tried to find a job with hours that would permit her to be home when her son came home from school each day. Her quest was daunting. Not only was a degree in Liberal Arts regarded as a 'negative' when considering an applicant's qualifications, (the choice of study having demonstrated a lack of foresight for eventual entry into the commercial job market) but by stipulating that she needed to be home no later than 3:30 p.m. each day, she further discouraged personnel managers from putting out their company's welcome mat. The supply of available jobs was somewhat limited.

Beryl, a Zen Buddhist and karate practitioner, was still doing part-time work when George proposed that they open a private investigation agency. Originally he had thought she would function as a "girl Friday" office manager; but when he witnessed her abilities in the martial arts, which, at that time, far exceeded his, he agreed that she should function as a 50-50 partner in the agency, and he helped her through the licensing procedure. She quickly became an excellent marksman on the gun range. As a Christmas gift he gave her a Beretta to use alternately with her Colt semi-automatic.

The Zen temple she attended was located on Germantown Avenue in a two storey, storefront row of small businesses. Wagner & Tilson, Private Investigators needed a home. Beryl noticed that a building in the same row was advertised for sale. She told George who liked it, bought it, and let Beryl and her son move into the second floor as their residence. Problem solved.

While George considered himself a man's man, Beryl did not see herself as a woman's woman. She had no female friends her own age. None. Acquaintances, yes. She enjoyed warm relationships with a few older women. But Beryl, it surprised her to realize, was a man's woman. She liked men, their freedom to move, to create, to discover, and that inexplicable wildness that came with their physical presence and strength. All of her senses found them agreeable; but she had no desire to domesticate one. Going to sleep with one was nice. But waking up with one of them in her bed? No. No. No. Dawn had an alchemical effect on her sensibilities. "Colors seen by candlelight do not look the same by day," said Elizabeth Barrett Browning, to which Beryl replied, "Amen."

She would find no occasion to alter her orisons until, in the course of solving a missing person's case that involved sexual slavery in a South American rainforest, a case called *Skyspirit*, she met the Surinamese Southern District's chief criminal investigator. Dawn became conducive to romance. But, as we all know, the odds are always against the success of long distance love affairs. To be stuck in one continent and love a man who is stuck in another holds as much promise for high romance as falling in love with Dorian Gray. In her professional life, she was tough but fair. In matters of lethality, she preferred *dim mak* points to bullets, the latter being awfully messy.

Perhaps the most unusual of the three detectives is Sensei Percy Wong. The reader may find it useful to know a bit more about his background.

Sensei, Beryl's karate master, left his dojo to go to Taiwan to become a fully ordained Zen Buddhist priest in the Ummon or Yun Men lineage in which he was given the Dharma name Shi Yao Feng. After studying advanced martial arts in both Taiwan and China, he returned to the U.S.

to teach karate again and to open a small Zen Buddhist temple - the temple that was down the street from the office *Wagner & Tilson* would eventually open.

Sensei was quickly considered a great martial arts' master not because, as he explains, "I am good at karate, but because I am better at advertising it." He was of Chinese descent and had been ordained in China, and since China's Chan Buddhism and Gung Fu stand in polite rivalry to Japan's Zen Buddhism and Karate, it was most peculiar to find a priest in China's Yun Men lineage who followed the Japanese Zen liturgy and the martial arts discipline of Karate.

It was only natural that Sensei Percy Wong's Japanese associates proclaimed that his preferences were based on merit, and in fairness to them, he did not care to disabuse them of this notion. In truth, it was Sensei's childhood rebellion against his tyrannical faux-Confucian father that caused him to gravitate to the Japanese forms. Though both of his parents had emigrated from China, his father decried western civilization even as he grew rich exploiting its freedoms and commercial opportunities. With draconian finesse he imposed upon his family the cultural values of the country from which he had fled for his life. He seriously believed that while the rest of the world's population might have come out of Africa, Chinese men came out of heaven. He did not know or care where Chinese women originated so long as they kept their proper place as slaves.

His mother, however, marveled at American diversity and refused to speak Chinese to her children, believing, as she did, in the old fashioned idea that it is wise to speak the language of the country in which one claims citizenship.

At every turn the dear lady outsmarted her obsessively sinophilic husband. Forced to serve rice at every meal along with other mysterious creatures obtained in Cantonese Chinatown, she purchased two Shar Peis that, being from Macau, were given free rein of the dining room. These dogs, despite their pre-Qin dynasty lineage, lacked a discerning palate and proved to be gluttons for bowls of fluffy white stuff. When her husband retreated to his rooms, she served omelettes and Cheerios, milk instead of tea, and at dinner, when he was not there at all, spaghetti instead of chow mein. The family home was crammed with gaudy enameled furniture and torturously carved teak; but on top of the lion-head-ball-claw-legged coffee table, she always placed a book which illustrated the elegant simplicity of such furniture designers as Marcel Breuer; Eileen Gray; Charles Eames; and American Shakers. Sensei adored her; and loved to hear her relate how, when his father ordered her to give their firstborn son a Chinese name; she secretly asked the clerk to record indelibly the name "Percy" which she mistakenly thought was a very American name. To Sensei, if she had named him Abraham Lincoln Wong, she could not have given him a more Yankee handle.

Preferring the cuisines of Italy and Mexico, Sensei avoided Chinese food and prided himself on not knowing a word of Chinese. He balanced this ignorance by an inability to understand Japanese and, because of its inaccessibility, he did not eat Japanese food.

The Man of Zen who practices Karate obviously is the adventurous type; and Sensei, staying true to type, enjoyed participating in Beryl's and George's investigations. It required little time for him to become a one-third partner of the team. He called himself, "the ampersand in *Wagner & Tilson.*"

Sensei Wong may have been better at advertising karate than at performing it, but this merely says that he was a superb huckster for the discipline. In college he had studied civil engineering; but he also was on the fencing team and he regularly practiced gymnastics. He had learned yoga and ancient forms of meditation from his mother. He attained Zen's vaunted transcendental states; which he could access 'on the mat.' It was not surprising that when he began to learn karate he was already half-accomplished. After he won a few minor championships he attracted the attention of several martial arts publications that found his "unprecedented" switchings newsworthy. They imparted to him a "great master" cachet, and perpetuated it to the delight of dojo owners and martial arts shopkeepers. He did win many championships and, through unpaid endorsements and political propaganda, inspired the sale of Japanese weapons, including nunchaku and shuriken which he did not actually use.

Although his Order was strongly given to celibacy, enough wiggle room remained for the priest who found it expedient to marry or dally. Yet, having reached his mid-forties unattached, he regarded it as 'unlikely' that he would ever be romantically welded to a female, and as 'impossible' that he would be bonded to a citizen and custom's agent of the People's Republic of China - whose Gung Fu abilities challenged him and who would strike terror in his heart especially when she wore Manolo Blahnik red spike heels. Such combat, he insisted, was patently unfair, but he prayed that Providence would not level the playing field. He met his femme fatale while working on *A Case of Virga*.

Later in their association Sensei would take under his spiritual wing a young Thai monk who had a degree in computer science and a flair for acting. Akara Chatree, to whom Sensei's master in Taiwan would give the name Shi Yao Xin, loved Shakespeare; but his father - who came from one of Thailand's many noble families - regarded his son's desire to become an actor as we would regard our son's desire to become a hit man. Akara's brothers were all businessmen and professionals; and as the old patriarch lay dying, he exacted a promise from his tall 'matinee-idol' son that he would never tread upon the flooring of a stage. The old man had asked for nothing else, and since he bequeathed a rather large sum of money to his young son, Akara had to content himself with critiquing the performances of actors who were less filially constrained than he. As far as romance is concerned, he had not thought too much about it until he worked on *A Case of Industrial Espionage*. That case took him to Bermuda, and what can a young hero do when he is captivated by a pretty girl who can recite Portia's lines with crystalline insight while lying beside him on a white beach near a blue ocean?

But his story will keep...

TUESDAY, JUNE 7, 2011

Although Mr. Steven Chang had been born and raised in Milwaukee, Wisconsin, he affected the deferential attitude of a peasant farmer in the presence of a mandarin. George Wagner felt uncomfortable. As he watched the man fumble with a loose button on his seersucker jacket and try to pinch a crease into his pants, speaking haltingly, without ever looking up, George was reminded of those old photographs of oriental men who were posed sitting up straight with both hands palm-down on their knees, fingers spread apart to show that none of their digits had been punitively removed.

Mr. Chang had been sitting on the chair beside George's desk for twenty minutes and the only information that George had squeezed from him was that his son was in serious trouble in Arizona. He had given the police a false name and was facing a second trial since the first one, which Mr. Chang had known nothing about, had ended in a mistrial. The words, "Tequila," "Papago," "murder," and "narcotics," seemed to escape from his mouth like stifled cries of pain.

"Mr. Chang," George spoke firmly, "when is the last time you had a good night's sleep?"

The question brought a response that further discomfited George. Mr. Chang burst into tears. He bent over and put his head down to his knees and sobbed. George took a box of tissues from a desk drawer and put it on the desk. Then he stared blankly out the window, waiting for the emotional storm to pass. When it did, the cop in George surfaced and he began to conduct the interview like an interrogation. "I'm going to ask you a few questions and I'd like you to answer them without any digressions. Just straightforward answers,

1

please. I'm going ask my partner - that lady in the front office - to sit in on this. I'll use this little digital tape recorder so that she won't have to take notes."

He went into the front office. "Help me out here," he whispered to Beryl. "The guy's emotional."

Beryl shut down her computer. "I know. I've been listening."

George introduced her to Mr. Chang and wheeled her desk chair back so that she could participate in the discussion. Before he continued the interview, he went into the back room kitchenette and brought three cans of iced tea from the fridge. "Now," he said, clicking on the recorder, "June 7, 2011, Tuesday, 11 a.m. Beryl Tilson and George Wagner interviewing Mr. Steven Chang who is inquiring about investigative help for his son--?"

"Adam."

"Adam Chang was charged with a crime in Arizona. When?"

"July 6th, 2010."

"What crime was Adam charged with?"

"Two counts of premeditated murder and trafficking in narcotics. I don't know the exact words. I never saw any of the original documents. I didn't know anything about the charges."

George's eyebrows arched and his eyes stared uncomprehendingly at Steven Chang. "Why the hell not? Those are serious charges!"

Mr. Chang shuddered a concluding sob. He cleared his throat, took a deep breath, and sighed resignedly. When he again spoke he no longer seemed obsequious. He spoke rather as a defeated man who had realized finally that nothing he could say or do would make the slightest difference in his fate. "He didn't want his mother and me to know about the trouble. He didn't think they could make the charges stick so he pleaded poverty, and the judge appointed an attorney to represent him. My boy wasn't granted bail so he sat in jail for eight months until his trial."

"How old is your boy?" George's tone insinuated that only a child or perhaps a young man who was intellectually impaired could possibly imagine that he didn't need to tell his parents, as if his crime had been pilfering somebody's lunch money. "You say that he didn't want to tell you or his mother. Where did you think he was during those months?"

George's attitude offended Mr. Chang. He opened his wallet and produced a group of photographs which he laid on the desk like playing cards. "My son graduated from Duke University. Here is his yearbook photo, and these were taken at his graduation ceremony. You can see my son, my wife and me, and also his partners who came to the ceremony. He was in business with them. He was doing research for the business when he was arrested. He's not a fool. He was naive in that childlike way that innocent people have when they can't imagine the kind of evil that's arrayed against them."

George put his hand up. "Give me a minute to look at these." He pushed the photographs towards Beryl. "Fine looking boy, you've got. Please go on."

"My son has a degree in Biology and Chemistry. He wrote to us and never mentioned that he had been charged with a crime. Yes... he lied. My wife has a serious heart condition. He was trying to spare her. He told us he wouldn't be able to communicate regularly with us for an indefinite period of time. He said he would be confined, living in a biosphere experiment. I know how stupid that sounds, but that was his field: Biology. He sent letters to someone who mailed them to us so that the Pima County Detention Center stamp wouldn't be on the envelope."

Beryl studied the graduation photographs, particularly the one of Adam standing between his two partners. One young man was tall and slim and dark haired, the other blonde and of Adam's height and build. Adam was holding up a piece of cardboard on which the words "Tres Amigos" was written. "Does this 'Tres Amigos' have anything to do with his business?" she asked.

"Yes. That's the name of it. Tres Amigos Old Spirits. They liked the TAOS acronym."

"What was he doing for the Tres Amigos company when he was arrested?" she asked.

"Getting samples of agave plants that grew there near the Mexican border. They were going to ferment and distill agave or mezcal. I don't know what it is. My son invented a new process that would remove the stuff that gives a person hangovers or something. I really don't know much about it. But they had started a legitimate business. The police wouldn't believe him, and he didn't want to give his real name. He thought they'd just let him go because the charges were so far fetched."

George wanted to know more about the victims. "Who were the two murder victims?"

"Nobody knows."

"What?"

"There were two men. They had no identification on them. They could have been reservation Indians, or Mexican nationals, or ordinary U.S. citizens. They were dead and no one could hear if they had an accent or ask them where they were from."

George suppressed a desire to laugh. "Funny how that is with dead people, so unwilling to share." He supposed that such a bizarre story had to be filled with misinformation, those half-truths and exaggerations that usually accompany denials of complicity. It could take months of frustrating work to separate truth from fiction. However genuine Mr. Chang's misery was, his problem would be more cheaply solved by Arizona private investigators. Still, he wanted to hear more of the bizarre tale. "So what happened at his trial?"

"He got a break. The judge declared a mistrial. Just as they were giving closing arguments, four different jurors met privately with the judge to tell him that they had been approached by a reporter and offered money for their story. The assumption was that my boy was going to be found guilty and their story about 'border' justice would make them rich and respected. A book was in the works, and a movie might be made of the book."

"One juror would have been bad enough, but four? Did they find the reporter?" George asked.

"No."

"You said he sat in jail for eight months," Beryl noted. "When did the first trial occur?"

"March 15 and 16, 2011."

"Two days? It should have taken that long to pick a jury. Where specifically did the crime occur?"

"Close to the Mexican border, in a little town called Las Flores, near the boundary of the Papago Indian Reservation, only it's not called that now. It has an Indian name." Chang again opened his wallet and removed a piece of paper, "Tohono O'Odham Nation."

"And he was charged with murdering two John Does. How were they killed?"

"With a .38 caliber Smith and Wesson revolver."

"Did your son ever own a gun of any kind?" George asked.

"None that I ever knew about."

"Where was he tried?"

"They took him to Tucson for the trial. Other than that he spent some of the eight months in the jail of a border-crossing town called Sasabe and some of it in the jail at Las Flores. They kept him near where the crime occurred in case somebody would identify the victims or recognize Adam's relationship to them, and they'd know how to proceed with a trial. It makes a legal difference whether the men were citizens, or members of an Indian nation, or foreign nationals. Nobody was anxious to prosecute the case until they knew the nationality of the dead men. At least that's what I understand. They waited for somebody to file a missing person's report, but no one did. I guess they figured that no matter what nationality they were, they were still drug traffickers so why waste time and money on them."

George shook his head. "No. In narcotics, there's also the possibility that the men were Mexican or U.S. undercover agents. What happened at the trial?"

"It was over in two days. Then they took Adam back to Las Flores to await the retrial. Adam was just *confused*. The case against him was more serious than he expected."

George grunted. "How did narcotics figure into the murders?"

"One of the men had a note in his pocket. It was in Spanish. I copied it down." He opened the paper on which he had written the Indian nation's name. "The note shows in numbers, '$750,000.' And then it says, '*No dar nada hasta que se cuente el dinero.*' This means, 'Give nothing until you count the money.'"

5

Beryl asked, "Adam was charged on July 6th. On what day did the crime occur?"

"July 5th. He was arrested there on the stretch of desert where the two men were shot. There was cocaine residue on the men, but there was no money. It was the same with my son. Cocaine residue in his car and no money."

Beryl interrupted. "Not the same. They had cocaine residue on them and that would tend to establish that they handled the cocaine. If his person was examined for traces of cocaine and they found none, that would tend to indicate that he had not handled the cocaine - especially since it was packaged in such a way that the other men got dusted with it. Was his person tested for cocaine residue?"

"I don't know."

"Were the drugs or money recovered?"

"No. They said that Adam had hidden the drugs somewhere in the desert. He didn't have the drugs or the gun on him when he was arrested."

"If he shot them he would have had residue from the gun fire on his hand and arm. Were they tested?"

"I don't know."

George nodded. "We'd have to have this answered... if we take the case."

Beryl wanted to know more about the re-trial. "The first trial was over in March. When is the next one scheduled?"

"July 11th."

The news was alarming. "What has been happening since March that it has taken you so long to seek help?" she asked.

"It just got so complicated."

George changed the subject. He did not want Mr. Chang to retreat into tears. "I'm curious, Mr. Chang. Who sent you to us?"

"My wife does light housework, mostly running errands, for an invalid lady who raises orchids. That lady told a friend who visits her regularly and knows you from the Orchid Society. She recommended you."

"I don't get to the meetings very often. Do you know the friend's name?"

"Smith. Mrs. Smith. That's all I know her by."

George's attitude immediately changed. "I know who she is. Cecilia Smith. A nice lady. Yes, a nice lady." He did not say that her daughter was the only star that shone, however distantly, in his romantic firmament.

Beryl asked, "The court appointed defense attorney - will he represent Adam at the second trial?"

"Yes and no. When the mistrial was called, a reporter named Dan Guest - he said he was freelance - came to my dry cleaning store and asked me for a comment. Comment? I didn't know anything about it!"

George protested. "I don't understand. You would have turned up in any background check. Nobody gets charged with felonies of this nature but that he's checked through various forensic data banks."

"He didn't have any identification on him; and he wasn't going to volunteer his name. He had never been arrested before and he said he 'wasn't in the system.' So he gave them the name 'Aaron Chin.'"

"What happened to his wallet and gas credit card receipts?" Beryl asked.

"This is where it gets complicated," Chang said wearily. He put his elbow on the desk and cradled his forehead in his hand.

"I'm glad it hasn't been complicated up to now," Beryl murmured.

Chang ignored the remark. "He had hashish in a bag under the seat. It was for his own private use, but there was a lot of it. He had just seen two men shot! A helicopter appeared out of nowhere and was chasing him, ordering him through a bullhorn to stop, and someone in the chopper began shooting at him. He pulled the bag of hashish out from under the seat and put it, his cellphone, his wallet, and anything else he had into a trash bag he always kept up front and tossed it into the desert. But once the news got out, people came from all around to look for the $750,000 and the drugs all that money was supposed to buy. We figure they found the bag."

Beryl was puzzled. "But what about the car he was driving? Was it a rental? He'd have had to give identification to get the car. Did he own it? They could easily trace the plates."

"My wife and I gave him the car. It was a graduation present, a two year old red Mustang we bought in a private sale in Trenton. He always wanted a Mustang. I gave the seller cash and he gave us a signed title. He was selling it for a friend. He said he'd see to it that the insurance stayed in effect for another three months to protect the registered owner in case Adam had an accident before he registered it. That's all I know. Private sellers don't give you much information. Adam said he couldn't afford to register it right away. If they did contact the last recorded owner, he probably wouldn't have known Adam's name."

"If Adam was conducting research for the Tres Amigos why didn't his business partners come to his assistance?" George asked.

"He didn't want to involve his associates in case the police found the hashish. He also didn't want to involve them in a murder and a drug trafficking incident. He thought it would be over in a few days."

George held up his hands. "How did the reporter know how to contact you?"

"After the mistrial was declared, a reporter wanted to write a story about the case. He convinced my boy to tell him who he really was. Adam knew I had borrowed money to pay his school expenses, and the reporter promised him that he'd give me a chunk of the proceeds from the book deal. And then this reporter, Dan Guest, filled me in with all the details and the names of the people who were involved... the deputy sheriff, the public defender, and so on. I called them but I didn't get anywhere. Dan said that if I wanted my boy to see the outside of a prison, I should get a first rate lawyer. He gave me the name of a lawyer in Chicago. I called his office but a secretary quoted me a retainer fee that was just too high. Then I flew down to the Las Flores jail and could barely recognize my own son. He lost so much weight and looked so haggard. 'Daddy,' he said to me, 'I didn't kill anyone and I don't know anything about cocaine or drug money. I am so sorry I brought this disgrace on you and momma.' He didn't ask for my help." Tears again welled in his eyes.

Beryl pushed the tissue box closer to him. "Tell us more about this business he was in."

"He and two of his acquaintances formed the company. One of them had inherited land which was filled with some special agave plants. The second partner bought a small distillery in Mesquite, Nevada, that had gone bankrupt. Adam had patented a filtration process that removed toxins and also let the stuff taste good. And then the two drug men were killed and the agave land became one big crime scene, and everybody was losing money waiting for this trial to be settled, and my boy was turning into a skeleton. So I hired the Chicago lawyer.

"My wife and I sold everything to give them the $200,000 they wanted to get started. But then we couldn't pay them any more after that money was used up. We were being charged for a staff to fly down to Tucson, stay in a nice hotel, eat, rent cars. They brought down their private investigator and he spent a lot of money re-photographing the site and re-interviewing people. We told the lawyer we were broke and everybody went back to Chicago, with the exception of one new lawyer who was fresh out of law school.

"The public defender, whose name was Harrison Metcalf, was a snooty kid from Flagstaff, Arizona, who didn't get along with the Chicago lawyer. The State required that a licensed Arizona attorney be there. The Chicago lawyer says he'll be back for the trial.

"As to your fee, I've gotten a good job with a former competitor of mine so I can pay you on the installment plan. I should add that Mrs. Smith said that if I truly believed my boy was innocent, you two would prove it and that if I couldn't afford you, she would pay your fee."

George shook his head. "That's kind of her, but we'd never let her pay. With me it's personal. I'm a close friend of a member of her family. All right, Mr. Chang, we'll work it out. There are ways we can economize if the defense attorneys are cooperative. My partner spent a few years in Arizona in the Phoenix area. Do you have to go to work now?"

"Not until 3 p.m."

"How about if you and Ms. Tilson here get started with the names and addresses of everyone you know who's connected to the case. I've got a one o'clock appointment but I'm leaving you in better hands than mine. If you get hungry, you can nuke some TV dinners in the back. We'll try to make this case as economical as possible."

Until two o'clock Steven Chang supplied all the details he could recall. As he left to get the bus to go to work, Beryl began the investigation in earnest. She verified background data and then placed a call to Public Defender Harrison Metcalf.

The receptionist coldly informed her that Mr. Metcalf was away on assignment and wouldn't return for a month. "I thought he had a trial scheduled for July 11th," Beryl said.

"I can't discuss Mr. Metcalf's schedule," the receptionist said, "but if you tell me the name of the client, perhaps there is another attorney who is handling the case."

"It is Adam Chang, a.k.a. Aaron Chin."

"You can try his criminal attorney. I think you'll find him in his Chicago office." She gave Beryl a phone number. "Is there anything else?"

"You could tell me his name" Beryl tried to sound 'matter-of-fact' and not sarcastic.

"Oh, sorry. It's Martin Mazzavini," she replied.

Beryl thanked her and called Mazzavini. She had to tell his secretary her name, business affiliation, and purpose of the call before the secretary would ask her boss if he would care to speak to her. Ten minutes after her call was first answered, Beryl heard the voice of Martin Mazzavini. She ordered herself to be patient and cooperative.

"Hello there, Ms. Tilson. I hear we have Adam Chang as a client. What can I do for you?"

"I'd like to look over the crime scene and the lab reports and see what we're up against by way of evidence against him. I called Harrison Metcalf but he's on assignment somewhere."

"The Southern Alps."

"I beg your pardon?"

"He's skiing in the Southern Alps. He goes every year."

"But what about the trial next month?"

"He'll fly in for it, I'm sure."

"And what about you?"

"Oh, I'll be there. But tell me, who engaged you?"

"Steven Chang, Adam's father."

"He surfaced? We've been looking for him. He disconnected his phone service and the mail we sent came back."

Again, Beryl reminded herself to remain non-judgmental. "He's somewhat distraught. He's had to sell his home, his car, his business, to raise the money to pay your fee. I suppose that he was so unused to being in abject poverty that notifying the post office slipped his mind."

"Ahhh. Do you have a personal connection to him?"

"If you're asking how he's going to pay us, he's not. It's not exactly pro bono. His wife works for a woman who has a friend who was once a client of ours. She recommended us. My partner is emotionally attached to the family. She offered to pay but George... George Wagner, my partner, won't take her money. So we're picking up the tab for 'old time's sake,' so to speak. Steven Chang is insolvent."

"You interviewed Steven Chang at length?"

"He just left my office. Yes, we talked for several hours. I learned a lot I'd like to check out."

"My secretary just put the file on my desk. Give me a moment," he asked, "to review this."

Beryl said nothing while she heard him mumbling as he read and turned pages.

"Well," Mazzavini finally said, "if you think you can shed some light on this troublesome case you ought to interview Adam for yourself and see the crime scene and all the photographs, and the trial transcript. We've also got a copy of a journalist's video recording that was admitted into evidence at trial. It shows the sheriff's recovery of the murder weapon just about where a witness reported he saw it being thrown. That was moments before Adam's red Mustang was overtaken by a pursuing police helicopter. Ummm... He gave a false identity: Aaron Chin. It wasn't until after the trial that his real name, Adam Chang, was learned. The Mustang wasn't registered to either name. Ummm... There is also a chemical analysis which showed cocaine residue in the back seat of his car. He also had several knives ranging in size from scalpels to machetes, syringes, test tubes, and plastic bags in his car, which I'm sure you'll agree are not items the average tourist would have."

11

Beryl restrained her rising anger. "But a biologist looking to sample the agave plants that grow there for the specific contents of their juice *would* have knives, syringes, test tubes, and plastic bags."

"He claimed he was a biologist, but he wouldn't give any supportive evidence, and nobody seems to have believed him."

"Adam Chang has a bachelor's degree in science from Duke University."

Mazzavini was startled. "Duke? Nobody told *me* that. Are you sure about this?" he challenged.

"Me, you question? This whole ridiculous scenario you accept; but me... you question? Has anyone called you a gullible fool lately? How did your last pyramid club membership work out? Am I on another planet? I, an unpaid worker, who heard the name Adam Chang for the first time today, am telling you, his two hundred thousand dollar attorney, that he is, indeed, a Duke graduate, class of 2010. His picture is in the yearbook and I've seen photos taken at the graduation ceremony... photos of him, his mom and dad and business associates. And, naturally, I verified this with Duke. Yes, he is in fact a botanist. He won a science contest in high school and was awarded an academic scholarship to Duke."

Mazzavini noted Beryl's anger. He softened his tone. "I apologize for my lack of... information. I'm assuming Metcalf knows all this. Maybe it's in the file and I missed it. Why did he lie about his name? That didn't help."

"Adam Chang lied, but he wasn't trying to deceive. His mother has a serious heart condition and he actually believed that the prosecution would drop the matter. According to his father, he was certain that he'd be released once the police understood that he was a biologist, which ultimately he could prove, and not a murdering drug trafficker, which ultimately no one could prove because it simply wasn't true. That, no doubt, is a philosophical distinction, not a legal one. Nevertheless, in consideration of his mom and his partners, he gave a false name and assumed that since the charge was so absurd it would just evaporate. He had no idea that the theory's greatest proponents would be his own attorneys. Didn't anybody in your office interview him?"

"Of course. Apparently, he wasn't coherent. He kept talking about tequila and some invention of his that was going to turn ordinary stuff into champagne or something. He didn't know anything about cocaine, yet, cocaine was found in his car. He was worried about money. Evidently Mr. Metcalf let it slip that my firm did not come cheaply."

"His ravings, while incoherent to you, were an accurate summation of his business and the reason he was on that land at the time of the crime. He and his partners were in the alcoholic beverage business. They were going to put those agave plants through a filtration process Chang had patented. I don't want to be impertinent, but what exactly did your firm accomplish 'defense-wise'?"

Martin Mazzavini laughed. "No matter how you ask it, that's sort of impertinent." He sighed. "Let me see. Well, we immediately reviewed the evidence, but there were problems. Metcalf acted as though he won the case when it was simply declared a mistrial. When my associates finally were retained - that was mid-April - Metcalf was leaving for Easter holiday. He had neglected to tell us that he'd be gone for two weeks. We had blocked in the time and then had to reschedule. So our involvement didn't occur until nearly mid-May. When a client begins his re-trial process by telling you that he lied about his name and never gave his attorney the names of anyone who could verify the reason he said he was in the area, and then starts raving about tequila, things have not gotten off to an auspicious beginning. Despite that, we did not abandon him. I met with him after his father ran out of money." He turned a page. "Oh, just a minute! I see that the drug charges were dropped in April. He's being held on murder charges only."

Beryl's anger could no longer be restrained. Her voice grew from a sinister hiss to a huckster's shout. "Do you know that there isn't a barber in the universe who isn't more informed about his customer than you are about your client? And all a barber has to worry about is a goddamned cowlick. This boy is on trial for his life! His father has gone bankrupt paying for your services. And when I, on his behalf, try to find out where things are standing legally, *I get told about the Southern Alps and that Oops! you just realized that half the charges were dropped.*" She composed herself.

"So just how far has your high-priced firm gotten preparing for the new trial? Made a few dinner reservations in Tucson? Mr. Mazzavini, I have never before encountered such an incompetent bunch of twits!"

"O-M-G. O-M-G," he said playfully, trying to lighten the discussion. "Please don't make that plural. Twit. I stand guilty. I don't blame you for being annoyed. I'd be annoyed too. This notice was stuck in the file. Perhaps I was away from the office. I don't know why I wasn't informed. I'll ask my secretary. Maybe I should fire her. Ok. I'll definitely fire her. Well, Miss Tilson, if I may call you that, you have to understand that Adam Chang is not easy to defend. When I went down there, Metcalf took me to meet him in the jail in a place called Las Flores, near a border town called Sasabe. He acted like he didn't give a shit one way or the other. He had that 'What's the use?' attitude. He did not care to be informative."

Beryl took a deep breath. "Let's start again. What about motive? What was the prosecution's theory of the crime?"

"Just that he had a rendezvous with two cocaine smugglers and rather than pay them, he killed them and helped himself to the cocaine. It happens all the time."

"He said a helicopter came out of nowhere and pursued him. He was in a desert not a Kansas meadow. He wasn't driving a four-wheel drive vehicle. It was an ordinary passenger car. He could not have gone off-road. That means he had to stay on the wheel ruts that pass for a trail. Are you getting this? He was set up... framed by the police for some reason. Didn't it strike you a little strange that a man was arrested at the scene of the crime and the police found no money, drugs, or weapon on him? Where could he have ditched the drugs or money? The police never found anything except the murder weapon... the next day. Did they test him for gun shot residue? He asked them to. *Did they?*"

"Please calm down. I don't know. That may have had something to do with the mistrial and why the drug charges were dropped. I'm not the most experienced attorney around, and when I first looked at the transcript and reviewed the evidence, it didn't seem kosher to me either. I couldn't get up to speed on it because co-counsel goes someplace for Memorial Day and then he leaves for his annual vacation in New Zealand. Apparently, he is well connected. We weren't technically retained until May, and this is only June. *Cut me some slack here!*" He pleaded, "Look, I planned to fly down to Tucson on the 23rd. But if you'd like to look things over I'll happily meet you there this Thursday if that's ok with you. Can you be there on Thursday?"

"Yes."

"Then let me make a peace offering to you. I'll fly you from... where are you?"

"Philadelphia."

"I knew that. I was testing you. And I'll rent a car and reserve rooms in a nice place that I stayed in before. You'll like it. I'll have the flight information sent to you immediately. Ok? I'll meet you in Tucson on Thursday." He joked, "Should I wear a red carnation in my lapel?"

"Yes... and tell them to put rosary beads in your hands."

"Ah, yes," Mazzavini said with mock seriousness, "they'll give my hands something constructive to do when the lid is closed."

Beryl continued to make phone calls about Adam Chang's case and also to rearrange her schedule.

Through a quick internet search for Tres Amigos Old Spirits, she located one of Adam's partners, Enrique Montoya, who lived in Santa Fe, New Mexico. A houseboy called him to the phone.

Montoya sounded both pleasant and concerned. "Adam was on my land when he was arrested. I feel responsible. I didn't know anything about his first trial until it was over. I learned about the second trial a few days after the mistrial was called."

"How did you find out?"

"A reporter contacted me. I can't remember his name. Guess, possibly?"

"Dan Guest?"

"Yes, that's it. Dan Guest. He came here to Santa Fe and met me for lunch. I was shocked. So was Ivan when I told him. Adam and I and another gentleman named Ivan, Ivan Onegin, had formed a mezcal distillery business in Nevada."

"The Tres Amigos?"

"Yes. Ivan purchased a small distillery plant and a new box truck to transport the harvested agave that grew on my land. He lost a considerable amount of money."

"What happened to the *Tres Amigos?*"

"We dissolved it, naturally. Adam was supposed to contact us in June of last year. He was doing additional testing on plants that grew at a higher elevation - plants that he suspected were genetically different from the others. We waited and waited and when we didn't hear from him we called his father and learned that Adam was participating in a biosphere experiment. At first we were angry, but then we contacted people at the EPA and several universities in the Southwest. Nobody knew anything about Adam and a biosphere project. We didn't want to upset his father since Adam had obviously lied to him. But without Adam's distillation process, there was no future for the business. We had to salvage what we could."

"And you never went to look for him on the land?"

"Ivan did. It would be impossible to find him if he were only a man on foot; but Adam drove a bright red Mustang. Ivan drove the entire length of the road that borders the land and there was no Mustang there. We checked the hospitals, which was a waste of time since we later learned that he hadn't been using his real name."

"What happened when you learned about the mistrial?"

"When the reporter showed up? I had never even considered drug trafficking so my first response was pure shock. Then, as he spoke, he referred to Adam's 'ongoing drug trafficking' and I knew there was no way Adam could have participated in any protracted drug operation *on my land*. He had been on the land only once before, in '08, while he was still in school. When we met Adam, we got to talking about making alcoholic spirits. I told him about the agave on my land. He had been considering a new way to ferment and distill agave, and I invited him to look at my land. When he saw acres and acres of this different strain of agave, he really went to work. I hired a fellow from Tucson to cut samples for him to work with. He didn't set foot on my land again, not that I know of anyway, until the time he was arrested. When we learned what had happened, just a few months ago, Ivan and I immediately went to Tucson and were told Adam, or Aaron, was in a jail in Las Flores. When we got there we were told he had just been moved. So we never did see Adam. We immediately informed the authorities of the precise nature of our association. Naturally, we offered to testify at the retrial."

"Which authority did you call?"

"The name eludes me at the moment. But if you speak to Adam, please convey our regards."

"If I may... would you tell me more about the creation of this business? It's such a strange story."

"The land is a small part of what had been a land grant to my family made back in the old *Encomienda* system. The Aztecs had many horticultural experiment stations and this particular parcel was dedicated to the improvement of pulque, the drink made from fermenting the agave plant. So they tried a variety of species in a form of hybridization. My great grandfather said that the agave plants that grew there now were the result of these experiments. There had once been orderly rows of them, but now they grew haphazardly. Perhaps natural selection and the pollen of other species had altered them. We had no way of knowing.

"No one had ever seen any value in the wild plants, but when Adam mentioned his new filtration system, we thought we saw opportunity's window open. I showed him the agave plants, and he put them through his process. It was as smooth a drink as you'll find. But when we realized that the window, for whatever reason, had been shut, we had to cut our losses. The disappointment was terrible. Even thinking about the land makes me ill."

The offhand way Montoya had said, "for whatever reason," convinced Beryl that she was not getting the whole truth. "Whatever reason" included the possibility of drug trafficking. Something was wrong. If Adam's filtration system had been so vital to their investment, they would have been on that land within hours of being unable to reach him by cellphone. They knew he was alone in the desert, traipsing around "higher elevations." He might have fallen. The land would have been the

17

first place they looked or sent law enforcement to look. And they wouldn't have waited months to do it. "You still had the land, but I suppose Mr. Onegin lost his investment. Did you have partnership insurance?"

"I'm certainly not going to discuss Mr. Onegin's losses with you. You'll have to speak with him yourself."

"Can you tell me where to reach him?"

"Actually, no. Ever since the agave debacle and the end of *Tres Amigos* we've not been in touch. He had moved around quite a bit before. But it's a fairly unusual name. You shouldn't have any trouble locating him. Please give my regards to Adam when you see him. It was very nice talking to you."

Before Beryl could respond, he said "Ciao" and hung up.

Ivan Onegin was more common a name than she had imagined. But one listing drew her attention. There was an Ivan Onegin in Scottsdale, Arizona, which lies on the eastern side of Phoenix.

She called the number. A housekeeper answered. Beryl determined from her tone and her reference to "Mr. Onegin" that she was a servant. But Mr. Onegin was not at home and she could not state when he was last at home or when he was expected to be next at home. It was the policy of the house not to discuss the residents' movements.

The anger Beryl felt when talking to Martin Mazzavini lingered in her mind. "I am calling from Philadelphia," she said. "It would be nice if you could give me some kind of clue. Should I call back in an hour? A day? Next month? And would you mind verifying that I am calling the correct Ivan Onegin? Handsome. In his twenties."

There was a long pause. Finally the housekeeper said, "Yes, that sounds like Mr. Onegin. Perhaps he will be here next month. I doubt that he will be here sooner, but I cannot be certain."

Beryl, trying hard to be civil, thanked her.

THURSDAY, JUNE 9, 2011.

Martin Mazzavini met Beryl at the airport. He was exactly what she expected. Well dressed, trim, about twenty-eight years old, black wavy hair and a nice complexion. Designer sunglasses shielded his eyes, but in the terminal when he called her name and she looked around, he quickly took the glasses off. "Nice touch," she said, shaking his hand. "Eye to eye contact."

He laughed. "It's all part of the presentation."

The rooms he had reserved were in the Arroyo Motel in Sahuarita, south of Tucson and north of Las Flores. Mazzavini had rented an SUV, and as they drove, they talked about their personal lives. He preferred the beauty of "Sherwood Forest" scenery. She loved the apparent barrenness of the desert. He had been engaged once but that was over and he never married. She was a widow with a son in college. She had attended a state college; he was a Cornell grad. He had never lived anywhere that wasn't a city or a city suburb. She had spent ten years in the desert near Phoenix.

The rooms were unquestionably the best rooms in the motel. They were at the northeast end of the single floor building. They were adjoining, both had French doors that opened onto a common patio, and were quiet since they were the farthest rooms from the highway. Only a narrow alley ran on the other side of the patio's high wall. As they checked in, Martin, in an exaggerated act of gallantry, had asked the clerk which of the two rooms was nicer, and then he insisted that Beryl be given that room. He pulled both of their rolling suitcases down the corridor, and as they arrived at her door, he deftly inserted her keycard and got the green light to blink on the first attempt. "Now," he asked, pushing the door open, "would a twit be this gentlemanly?"

"Guys who hang out in motels are good at opening doors. You were pretty good. Too bad Adam Chang isn't being held prisoner on the patio."

"Aarrgh," he said, continuing down to his door.

"There's a key in the lock of the connecting doors," Mazzavini said. "Do you want to keep it?"

"No. Leave the door unlocked. The easy access is for safety not for intimacy."

"Why safety?"

"Because *we know* that our client is innocent and that means that someone else is guilty. And that person might not appreciate our poking around, trying to discover his identity."

"I hadn't considered that," he said. "Well, shall we sit outside at the patio table and review the transcript? How's iced tea and quesadillas sound?"

"Sounds fine," Beryl answered. "Give me five minutes. I want to hang my clothes in the bathroom."

Mazzavini stood in the shared doorway. "Why do you hang your clothes in the bathroom?"

"I hang them on the shower curtain rod. Then I run hot water in the tub and as soon as steam fills the room, I shut off the water, run out of the bathroom and shut the door behind me. And the steam takes the packing wrinkles out of the clothes."

"I'll have to remember that."

"For all those times that you don't have valet service."

Beryl kicked off her shoes and went out onto the patio and sat under an umbrella table. "Nice," she said. Water dripped sluggishly from a stone fountain and bougainvillea cascaded over the enclosing walls. Colorful plants bloomed in clay pots that were grouped in the corners. "Look at all this red," she said as she sat down. "Bougainvillea, hibiscus, geranium."

"I don't know one from the other. May I call you Beryl?" he asked.

Impulsively, Beryl imitated Kiefer Sutherland in *A Few Good Men*. "No *you may not!*" Before she could explain that she liked to quote the movie, he replied, imitating Tom Cruise, "*Have I done something to offend you?*"

"No. I like all you Navy boys." They both laughed.

"It's a disease," he said as he put the case files on the table.

The coroner's report indicated that two .38 caliber slugs had been recovered from each body. A diagram pinpointed the exact location of the entry points.

Beryl studied the report. "John Doe #1 was shot first," she said, "because he was shot head on, in a frontal attack. Two bullets entered the upper chest, left of sternum, between the 4th and 5th thoracic ribs. The bullets shattered the aorta. He died just about where he stood. Fast. But John Doe #2 had turned to flee and was shot in the side, the left upper outer quadrant. The bullets got his spleen, kidney, and also his aorta. He didn't get very far either. Four shots total."

"That would seem to be the case. Two drug mules facing an armed man. Curious."

"Same bullets. Same gun. One shooter. It happened fast. I'd like to see what John Doe #1 was wearing and also what kind of car or truck they were driving."

"Why?"

"Because *we know* Adam Chang did not shoot them so we must assume someone else did. As you noted, two guys don't usually just stand there unarmed in front of someone armed, not in such a big drug deal, anyway. If JD#1 had his hands up in the air, like, 'Put your hands up!' as a cop commands, the hole in the man will not match up with the hole in his outer garment. When a man raises his arms, the garment covering his chest rises. The bullet keeps going straight."

"Ok. And you want to know the kind of vehicle so that you can figure out what kind of garment he might be wearing. If it's air conditioned and new, he could have a heavier shirt on. If it's not air conditioned, he might even be bare chested."

Beryl examined the report. "That would be reasonable, but #1 wasn't bare chested. Wool? It says wool fibers and cotton fibers were embedded in the point of penetration. Maybe he was wearing a poncho."

"In July? Wouldn't he look stupid wearing a wool poncho in July?"

"Not necessarily. Moisture mitigates temperature extremes. A desert is a desert because it doesn't have moisture. When the sun goes down, it gets cold. Cold is also a function of altitude. What's the altitude of the crime scene?"

"Ahhhh. I don't know. I'll find out."

"It's odd that two veteran drug mules - they had to be veterans because rookies wouldn't be entrusted with that quantity of cocaine - would stand there and be shot by a gringo biologist they never saw before. I just hope the two of them weren't Mexican drug enforcement agents. You never know.

"John Doe #1 wouldn't necessarily look out of place wearing a poncho. If the air conditioning was set high to please the other guy, he might have felt cold. Also, if he wanted to conceal a weapon, he'd wear a poncho, maybe. Where is the evidence kept?"

"In the evidence room in Tucson." Mazzavini stood up. "Let me get my iPad to take some notes."

"Get a pencil and paper and write in as much abbreviation as possible. If you lose that iPad, you lose everything. People don't pay attention to little spiral tablets. But anybody... even someone who doesn't have an interest in the case may want your iPad."

"Ok, but I don't have a paper and pencil."

"Put your iPad in my tote bag inside my sweater. You'll find an extra paper tablet and pencil in there. By the way, do you have clothes that blend in?"

"I'm a lawyer, not a cow-poke. This ain't exactly cattle country. Why do you want me to blend in?"

"*What I do want is for you to stand there in your faggoty Armani suit and Cornell mouth...* "

"I get it. I get it. And how did you know my suit's Armani?"

"Because the label says so, right inside the jacket - the jacket you've hung on the back of the chair."

"Ok. Good. Shall we go shopping for western stuff? Levi's and cowboy boots?"

"Yes... but later. For now, let's keep on reading. We may find other things to do in Tucson in the morning. JD#1's garments. Altitude. And let's find out exactly how tall JD#1 was." She looked through the report. "168 centimeters. That should be about 5'6". As tall as I. I hope we don't have to dig this guy up."

"Without an exhumation order?"

"No. Let's just throw the idea out there until somebody objects and shows signs of worry. It would be nice to hear their reaction. I'm not going to tell you that I might tap phone calls if I get suspicious."

"I can get equipment to pick up a cellphone conversation."

"You can't have anything to do with spy ware. I'll buy any equipment I need. You can 'lend' me the money, cash, for 'personal' things I need. Look on the web to see precisely what it will cost. Make sure it records as well as listens. It will probably come with software that we can load into my laptop. We'll get it next time we go into Tucson. What I'd like to see is the record of his hands being tested for gun shot residue."

Martin flipped through a few pages, then looked up with a guilty expression. "I can't find it."

"For now, let's read on."

"Here," Martin said, "is the testimony of Wayne McPeak who lives on the west side of Sasabe Road... that's highway 286... and Nubes Road... which is a dirt road. Quote, 'I was eatin' my lunch on the front porch of my house. It was around twelve-thirty. I know that because my woman brings me my lunch after she watches a couple of them soap operas she likes. It was July the fifth. That was a Monday. I know that because we had been to a barbecue up in Diamond Bell on the Fourth of July and Jim and Nancy Domingues gave us one of them styrofoam boxes for take-out with a lot of leftovers she had. Friends of theirs couldn't make it down from Tucson and she had a lot of stuff left over so she give it to us. That's the kind of people the Domingues' are.'" Martin looked up. "Do you think that maybe there was a Domingues on the jury?" He began to laugh merrily.

Beryl couldn't help laughing, too... "Lay on, McPeak."

"So let's make a note. Wayne McPeak fixes the time at 12:30 p.m. on 7/5/10. The ADA, a female attorney evidently - since her name is Loralee Williams - asks that he tell the court what he saw and heard. Wayne replies, 'I was sittin' there eatin' - had my food on my lap - when I hear Bang Bang, Bang Bang, four shots, and I put my food down and stand up and look at the Montoya land where the shots come from. I see a red car headin' north leavin' a big cloud of dust and then I see a silver car take off after it, leavin' its own cloud of dust. There's a red truck parked back aways to the south, but it don't move... cause it's parked. You know what I mean?' (laughter) This guy is a stand up comic." Martin began to laugh again even more contagiously.

Beryl found herself shaking with laughter. "I don't know why this is so funny."

Martin continued. "'Then I see something silver come out of the red car. It makes an arc, like a looping fly to a third baseman... or maybe a bunt.' Why does he say a third baseman? Why not first or second?"

"Probably because he's got a baseball diamond oriented in his mind - he's got 'Diamond Bell' on the brain. Do a quick Google search and see where his house is located. I'll see if I can find the GPS location of the gun." Beryl found the information in a cover sheet for the video evidence. "I've got the gun's location at Latitude North 31 degrees, 29 minutes, 42 seconds. Longitude West 111 degrees, 33 minutes, 45 seconds. The gun was found at 2000 feet elevation. The land tops at 3600 feet."

Martin gave up the search on his iPhone. "Wayne's house doesn't show up. We can check it when we get there."

"What else does Wayne say?"

Martin resumed the testimony. "'I got out my phone and I called Deputy Garcia and told him about the gunshots and the two cars, and he tells me that the red car is trying to get away and the silver car is *his* car and he's in pursuit of the crook in the red car. I tell him that the guy in that red car threw somethin' silver into the desert. And the sheriff says that I should be sure to remember where I saw it cause this is one perp that ain't gonna get away.' And then Loralee asks him what he did next and he says, 'I got off the horn. Weren't no time to chew the fat.' Metcalf should have objected a dozen times. But what the hell? Saint Patrick's Day was only twenty-four hours away. He probably had a plane to catch to Dublin. And then Wayne says, 'Soon I could hear the helicopter but I didn't see or hear anything else until the coroner's van comes and collects two victims and the tow truck comes to take the red truck to the police evidence yard. I didn't go look because I didn't want to get in the way... I figured if there was something they needed from me, they knew where to find me. And the next day Deputy Garcia comes to my house and asks me if I remember where I saw the gun thrown.' That it was a gun he saw hasn't been established, but Metcalf doesn't object. 'He tells me they've got the guy and he wants to personally thank me for being a good citizen and callin' in when I saw a crime being committed.' Jesus! Metcalf still doesn't object. This is outrageous! 'So he sits down on my porch because we're gonna wait for a newspaper reporter to show up and go looking for the gun and also go to the yellow-taped crime scene where the bodies were. I guess they knew that where there was gunfire there was bound to be somebody smoked. (laughter).' I cannot believe what I'm reading."

"I thought you said you looked over the transcript?"

"'Looked it over' doesn't mean I read it."

"Apparently not. Go on."

"The judge objects to the attempt at levity. He reminds the witness that a young man is on trial for very serious charges. Wayne continues, 'We waited on my front porch and sure enough the newspaper guy shows up. I get in Deputy Garcia's car--' Wait! Wait! Wait just a minute! He says 'Deputy Garcia.' I looked at the list of law enforcement personnel who testified. I don't remember seeing any Deputy Garcia. Who the hell is Deputy Garcia?" Martin flipped through the pages until he found the testimony of Hugo Garcia, an owner of a long haul trucking company that brings Mexican vegetables and fruits into the U.S. via the Sasabe port of entry. "He resides at his ranch, the Hacienda Santa Caterina, near Las Flores, and serves his community as a member of CSLEP Civilian Support Law Enforcement Personnel. Jesus!" He flipped through more pages. "The arresting officer was a police Captain... Anthony Breyer. He was covering for several subordinates who had taken extended holiday time. He arrived in a police car. And the two men in the helicopter were also CSLEP volunteers. This is a revelation! Both the pilot and the guy with the bullhorn were not law enforcement officers. It doesn't give either of their names. Why the hell not?"

"And he never mentions testing Adam's hands for gun powder residue. Remember to check for that. Ok. Continue with Wayne."

Martin searched the pages until he found where he had left off. "'-and our two cars go into the desert to go look for the murder weapon. And we sees the buzzards circling round and we know somebody did some bleedin' out there.'"

"What time of day is this?"

"The camcorder will tell us." Martin Mazzavini went into his room and returned to the patio with his laptop. "Here it is in living color."

Beryl watched the screen. "The video was made on July 6, 2010, beginning at 12:20 p.m. Ok. There's no official law enforcement personnel there... just Citizen McPeak, Amateur Deputy Sheriff Garcia, a newspaper reporter and his cameraman."

Martin pointed to the figures on the screen. "There is Wayne and the reporter."

They let the video roll: the reporter says, "Tom Zawicky of the Morning Herald reporting." He turns to the deputy. "This is Deputy Hugo Garcia and Mr. Wayne McPeak." The deputy waves, turns away, and starts walking away from the camera. "Would you introduce yourself, Wayne?"

Wayne replies, "I'm just a guy doin' his civic duty. The name's Wayne McPeak." He salutes the camera lens and turns to join Deputy Sheriff Hugo Garcia.

The reporter takes the camera and resumes his narrative. "Pursuant to hearing four shots being fired on July 5th at approximately 12:30 p.m., Wayne McPeak called Deputy Sheriff Garcia, enabling him to stop the alleged suspect, Aaron Chin, before he could exit on Sasabe Road."

Martin looked up and shrugged. "That's not entirely true, but what the hell?"

The camera turns away to focus on the backs of the Deputy and Wayne McPeak. As he walks, Zawicky continues to narrate the activity. "Mr. McPeak reported seeing a silver object being thrown in the area towards which McPeak and Garcia are walking now." He calls to the Deputy, "Deputy Garcia, are you searching for the murder weapon at this time?"

"Yes, but keep your eyes open," Deputy Garcia calls. "Film anything that looks suspicious." He continues to walk ahead with Wayne McPeak as the camera pans the ground and then refocuses on the backs of Garcia and McPeak. Zawicky is about thirty feet behind them.

Suddenly McPeak stops and Garcia moves in front of him and bends over. The camera records McPeak beside a large agave plant and the bent-over back of the deputy. Garcia stands up and shouts, "Here it is! Come over here and get this!" The camera moves in a jerking motion as the cameraman jogs ahead beside Zawicky and approaches the two men. "Look at this!" Garcia says, pointing to a revolver that is lying on a bare patch of land. The camera stays on the gun, Garcia reads a GPS device, pulls a thin surgical glove on his right hand, and bends over to pick up the gun. He immediately holds it in front of the camera.

Zawicky asks, "Got a make and caliber on that gun, Deputy?"

Garcia puts his left palm over the barrel and grips the revolver as his right thumb brushes the frame's yoke, so that the Smith and Wesson SW circular logo can be seen. Then he pushes the cylinder release and flips open the cylinder and reads "Smith & Wesson, .38 caliber." He pushes the ejector rod and lets the 4 spent and 2 live rounds fall into his gloved hand. "Looks like it was just as Mr. McPeak said: 4 shots fired and we have two remaining." He turns to McPeak, "Lemme' get a bag." He reaches into his breast pocket and removes two folded plastic evidence bags.

The revolver is put into one bag and the bullets and casings are put into another. Garcia seals and signs the bags.

Zawicky asks, "Do you think you'll get any good prints off the gun?"

Garcia says, "No way. What you'll get is saliva from coyotes. They all come to see if it's edible and they slobber all over whatever they find especially if it's got a man's scent on it."

"Well," said Beryl, "there is your case. You can have your client acquitted or the charges against him dismissed outright. And then you can sit back and smile as perjury, plus murder, plus God knows what else, are brought against the deputy and McPeak, et al. And you can no doubt sue for a big big bunch of money for the damages Adam Chang sustained. And while you're at it, try to find out why they didn't dust the bullet casings. Or do they have coyotes that love the smell of gunpowder so much that they slobber over the inside of the cylinder?"

"And how am I going to prove all that? And please don't say, "*I have no idea*."

"Martin, there isn't a human being who has spent any time in the desert who will disagree with me. Nobody... absolutely nobody picks up a metal object that has lain in the July sun for hours. That sun was directly overhead. There were no shadows. Nothing protected that metal from heating up beyond any human flesh's ability to touch it - especially wearing a thin latex glove - really no more than a condom's covering. And he held the barrel right in the palm of his hand. That gun was put there within five minutes of the time it was filmed. Do you know that people keep potholders in their cars in case they park without having put a screen over the windshield and the sun hits the steering wheel. So they use potholders until the air conditioning kicks in. Since there is no way that a bare human hand picked up a hunk of metal that has been lying for hours in the July sun in the Sonora desert, the film that purports to show this is an obvious fake. Your client was set-up by McPeak and Garcia and the prosecution colluded in the perjury."

"This is all new to me. We just don't have the problem with the sun. Chicago's the 'windy city.'" Martin tried to sound convinced. "Potholders, hmmm. And I guess that if he was asked why he picked the gun up without regard for the fingerprints, he would say, 'Who else could any fingerprints belong to? McPeak saw him throw the gun away.' Ok, let's keep watching the video."

"No!" Beryl said emphatically, "I can tell that you still don't appreciate what I'm telling you. Let's go outside." She put her shoes on. "You parked in the open. Let's go see what we've got. Bring the car keys."

They locked the rooms and went out into the parking lot. The afternoon sun was shining on the windshield. "Open the car," Beryl said, "and sit down and grab the steering wheel."

The moment the door opened, a blast of hot air engulfed him. Beryl pushed him. "Go ahead! Grab the wheel!"

Martin's had touched the wheel and then recoiled. "Damn!" he yelled.

"And I left the window open slightly on my side. If I hadn't there's a good chance the heat would have cracked the windows. When that happens you get a windshield filled with fine spider web cracks. Or, if you had an aerosol can in here, it could have exploded. It sounds like a gunshot." She looked on the ground for a piece of metal trash that had been lying in the sun. Seeing a two-inch iron bolt lying in the gutter, she pointed to it and said, "Ok. Pick that up."

Again, Martin, still not entirely convinced, walked to the gutter and tried to pick it up. He touched it and immediately withdrew his hand. "Ok. I get it. It's hot."

"Do you have a condom in your wallet?"

Martin shook his head and complied. "I never even gave this heat situation a second thought." He took a condom from his wallet and tore the packet open. "You know what this means," he said slyly.

"Oh, my! Such a big condom! What a shame to waste it. Now put as much of your hand in there as you can and grab that bolt. Let's see you do it."

Martin squeezed his hand into the condom and, as if he thought the latex would afford his fingers some protection, he curled his fingers around the bolt. The latex melted. He flung the bolt to the ground and cursed the burn he had received. "I got it," he said as he pulled the condom off his hand. He looked around for a trash receptacle and, finding none, put the burnt condom in his pocket. "I got it loud and clear. That son of a bitch was putting on a show for the camera. *But why the hell didn't Metcalf see that?*"

"Remember, Metcalf is from Flagstaff. People ski in Flagstaff. Cold is a function of altitude and Flagstaff is high and cold. Maybe he's like a Chicagoan when it comes to things like this, or maybe he doesn't care enough to consider the validity of the evidence, or maybe he's in on the fix."

They returned to the room. "Shouldn't I get butter for my hand?" Martin asked.

"No. Just run cold water over it, right away."

"I hope you realize what your little experiment has done to my sex life. I am never going to be the same. Every time I use one of those things I'm gonna' remember this - this burning, melting latex. It will be the equivalent of a cold shower."

"On the other hand... well, not the other hand," she grinned, "your right hand will heal quickly and solve—" She had to turn her head away to keep him from seeing that she was laughing.

He groaned. "Is letting you rag me the tuition I have to pay?" Smiling, he went into his bedroom and at the bathroom sink he ran cold water over his hand. When he rejoined her on the patio, he said, "Ok. I've learned a lesson and I know, experientially, that the video admitted into evidence was bogus. But they declared a mistrial. This is a new trial and they may decide not to try to enter the footage as evidence."

"Since you know your client is innocent, you know that *any* so-called evidence they offer to prove his guilt is bogus. That's the premise you have to start with."

"But what about the next piece of evidence that's phony? There are all kinds of ways to cheat."

"You have to be aware at all times of the possibility of deceit. What is a weed? Answer that. What is a weed?"

"I don't know. A plant nobody wants. A worthless plant."

"No. It's a plant that is out of place. According to the design of its surroundings, it does not belong there. We notice it because there is something different about it. It is unusual. Something about it doesn't fit."

"I'll look for what's out of place. Ok. I got it."

"But you can't just trust appearances. You have to question everything. Look," Beryl said apologetically, "I know I was tough on you making my point about the temperature of metal in the desert sun. You needed to be completely convinced, and you couldn't be that until you experienced it for yourself. People see Hollywood movies. They see people with sweaty shirts in the hot desert. That's Hollywood. *All* people associate sweat with work, but only a *small number* of the people who view the film understand evaporative rates in the desert. You will not see sweat in the desert. Do you know what 'virga' is?" she asked.

"I'm not going to say, 'a constellation.' I know that that's Virgo."

"That's right. We want 'virga.'"

"No, I don't know what 'virga' is."

"Virga is ordinary rain or even snow that falls from the sky, but in the desert's heat, it does not reach the ground. Heat rises. The rain evaporates before it can reach the ground. It's the strangest thing to see. Look it up."

Martin hesitated. "I believe you."

"*Look it up!* If you don't understand the desert you're not going to get your innocent client acquitted. Look it up!"

Martin flicked through his smartphone and got the definition. He read it to himself. "I'll be damned. I never heard of virga before. Never. So it gets so hot on the ground that heat radiates upwards and the rain evaporates. It just burns off before it reaches the ground."

"And how hot do you think steel gets lying in the July sun in the Sonoran Desert? Look it up."

"Yes, Ma'am. I assume nothing." Beryl read through the trial transcript while Martin searched. In ten minutes he had the answer. "At 140 degrees Fahrenheit or 60 degrees Centigrade you're gonna get a second degree burn. And the ambient temperature can easily be 116 degrees. Lying in the sun, depending on many variables, can heat the metal up to 176 degrees or 80 Celsius. Jesus. Water boils at 212."

"Maybe when the judge or one of the jurors saw that video fakery a concern was voiced and the mistrial was called."

Martin Mazzavini put his hands up in the air. "I surrender."

"Now do you see how you've won your case?"

"What do we do now?"

"Go to a licensed lab or to the University and hire someone to put an exact duplicate of the weapon out in the sun at the exact place they filmed the other gun. Then record the temperature at increasing intervals and get a dermatologist to testify that the metal could not possibly have been picked up in the manner in which the deputy and McPeak claimed. Show that the exact kind of latex glove he used could not have protected his hand from the heat. It may have melted into the skin and caused more damage. You'll need someone to testify to the temperature on the day of July 6, 2010. Your experts will know what to do."

"Do you really see me winning my first murder trial?"

Martin's lack of self-confidence was disconcerting. "I don't get it. You appear to be so confident. But underneath all that 'presentation' you're tentative. I'm not trying to be insulting. I really want to know. You've got your name on what is supposed to be a really good firm. How did that happen? Is that some sort of gift from your dad?"

"I'm not one of the Mazzavinis in the firm's name. My grandfather's name is first on the letterhead. He founded the firm. He's the brains of the outfit. A great attorney and a great guy. He pronounces it the Italian way, Mattzavini, like Pizza. And my father is the other Mazzavini. The firm's name is Mazzavini O'Brian Mazzavini. MOM for short."

"I hesitate to ask. What will it be when your star rises?"

"If it ever does, the name won't change. My grandfather will retire."

"If? You doubt that your star will rise?"

"Frankly? Look at the mess I've made of this case. I went to school with guys who are making headlines. Last month I loused up a simple misappropriation case and my father shouts to my grandfather that he's getting me a new pair of running shoes for when I get good enough to chase ambulances."

"Ouch. Maybe you don't want your star to rise because it will mean your grandfather will be gone and you'll be there alone with your father." Beryl gathered the papers and laptop together and stood up. "Martin, you have everything: brains, charm, good looks, connections, and above all a certifying law degree from Cornell. You're like that Tom Cruise character. You know how to be a great lawyer. You just don't know how to be you. You're too burdened with Mazzavini expectations."

"Well, nobody expects me to do anything with this case. Maybe I'll meet myself. Can I take you and him to dinner? Are you hungry?"

"Yes... yes I am."

"I'm going to buy you the best steak in Tuck-son. Come on. We'll ask at the desk just where that steak can be found."

"Ok. But bring your laptop and camcorder and all the case material you brought with you. Don't leave anything in the room. As it says in the *Hagakure*, 'Tether even a roasted chicken.'"

Martin Mazzavini went to his suitcase and removed a few files and added them to the other case-related items he had gathered. "I did not carry an attaché case. It takes up half the suitcase and given a choice between crushing my Gucci shirts and ties and my Armani underwear, and bringing something as inconsequential as a trial transcript, I naturally deferred to the exigencies of the successful attorney's wardrobe. He took the plastic laundry bag from his closet and put all the case material inside. Slinging the bag over his shoulder he said, "Regardless of the personal cost to my self-esteem, your wish will forever constitute the principles, that is to say, 'the Code', I live by."

The desk clerk recommended a steak house and offered to call ahead for reservations.

They were seated in a booth in the restaurant. Beryl's tote bag was beside her on the seat and Martin's white laundry bag was beside him.

"Victory," pronounced Martin as he ordered a quality bordeaux, "is no longer a long-shot. It is now the favorite in the morning line."

Spirits were high as they dined on the best steak the restaurant had to offer.

As they waited for dessert, Beryl brought up Adam's agave distillation. "Enrique Montoya was pleasant enough, but I'm convinced he was giving me a lot of baloney. Three guys pool their resources and invest in a limited partnership for making mezcal. One guy has the raw material - the agave plants; the other guy has the physical plant for fermenting and distilling the material and also a new truck for transporting the raw material. The third guy has the process for converting the raw material into a very special finished product. The third guy is on desert land sampling some unusual species at the highest altitude it grows on that rocky terrain. They're anxious to get started making mezcal. But when the guy with the formula doesn't show up, they wait and wait and are much annoyed. They call his father and hear about the biosphere experiment and they really get mad. Then they find out there doesn't seem to be any biosphere project. One of them drives past the land and doesn't see a red Mustang, so they dissolve the partnership. Does that strike you as odd?"

"All three guys are vital to the production. Now that I've looked more closely at the desert around here, I'd never let one of my key personnel out there alone. I'd be in constant communication with him. Suppose he got hurt!"

"Oh, yes. And I asked Montoya if they had partnership insurance and he refused to discuss it. But there's more that's weird. They didn't hear that Adam was in jail until after his mistrial was declared. One year after they last saw him. Then they both went together to Las Flores to visit him. But he wasn't there so they talked to law enforcement and learned just how compelling the case against Adam was. Maybe they were colluding with those alleged law enforcement people. And Montoya said he didn't know how I could reach Ivan; and Ivan Onegin is a resident of Phoenix. This is truly bizarre. As of this moment they haven't seen Adam in a year and three months."

"It's got to be bullshit. I'll make a note to look into it right here in my new technological aid. Did you ever talk to Ivan?" He took his new small blue spiral tablet and made a dutifully cryptic note. "ck 3 amg hist & prtshp ins doc."

Beryl reached into her tote bag and made her own notes. "And no, I didn't talk to Ivan. He's supposed to be away someplace and may or may not be back next month. Mister Onegin's servants are not talkative people."

They lingered over Grand Marnier as Martin showed his notes to Beryl.

"Let's see if I can interpret them. "6/9/10 ck pnch bul hl. msr dwn frm shldr. 5'6" ; by shrt, pntz & bts. ; Ord lb ht tst mtl. ; wy no vst frm rk & ivn. get bkgrnd on rk & ivn. wy dislv 3 amgos so qwk. chk ptnr ins.

"June, nine, ten. Check poncho bullet hole. Measure down from shoulder. Five feet six inches. Buy shirt, pants and boots. Order lab heat test metal. Why no visit from Rick and Ivan. Get background on Rick and Ivan. Why dissolve Tres Amigos so quickly. Check partnership insurance.

"Will I be able to read your notes that easily?"

"Probably." They talked another half hour over coffee and, encouraged and confident about their first day of collaboration, they ended the discussion.

Then they drove back to the Arroyo Motel and discovered that their rooms had been ransacked.

Beryl called the desk clerk to report the break-in. When she hung up the telephone, she signaled Martin to say nothing. She motioned to him that they go outside to the parking lot.

"What have you learned from this, Counselor?" Beryl whispered.

"Don't leave stuff lying around."

"No. Somebody tipped off somebody. We don't know who and we don't know why. What we do know is that it's unlikely that anything we had with us was the target since everything we had exists elsewhere where it can legally be accessed and they already know that we don't have anything new. The Southern Alps and all that. Now, what is unusual about our rooms?"

"The patio."

"Yes. And what else? Think location."

"We're at the end of the building."

"Suppose somebody wanted to eavesdrop on our conversation. Could they park outside?"

"No. The alleyway is too narrow."

Beryl smiled. "What will happen next is standard. We'll be given a new pair of bugged rooms, assuming they have any available. And all our clothing and stuff will be moved into those rooms. And under a collar or the loop in some pants' pocket - in some hidden place - tiny little microphones will be placed. If we had left a cellphone in the room, it would now be bugged. And there will be a private frequency GPS beacon emanating from the undercarriage of our car.

"But outside the door, in some innocuous van there will likely be a guy recording our conversation. They'll want us in the same place, so probably they'll give me a really nice big room - maybe a double room

35

even - and you'll get a broom closet. The van will be outside my room and naturally you will spend more time there. So from here on in, we can't speak about the case in any meaningful way."

"They've probably bugged our car, too. So tomorrow when we get into the car to go shopping, you start an argument about wanting to buy some Indian pots and jewelry and you want to make a side trip. I'll say, 'No! I have too much work to do.' And I'll add, 'Nobody's stopping you from getting your own goddamned car.'"

"Good idea. Now you're thinking. We can leave the bugged car and rent a clean one. Then we can talk."

"And as to the burglary," Martin said, "it only looks like somebody tried to steal stuff. What are we going to report as a stolen item? Nothing's missing. So I guess that we'll go along with the charade and say we haven't been able to inventory all the stuff we had in the room. In the morning when we go to get new clothes at one of the western wear shops or Wal-Mart, we'll get some good spyware."

"Right."

Their possessions were moved into separate rooms, many rooms apart. Beryl's was large and next to the parking lot and Martin's was, as expected, small. After they were settled in, he came to her room and whispered, "I felt like bad weather had grounded me on a flight that stopped at Tokyo... like one of those overnight airline rooms they give you at Narita. I had to walk sideways to get around the bed."

FRIDAY JUNE 10, 2011

Since they no longer had adjoining rooms Martin's "wake-up" call came by way of Beryl's cellphone. She hoped that he would remember that it was more likely than not that they were being listened to. He remembered. "Are we going out to breakfast?" he asked.

"Sure," she said. "But with the burglary's confusion last night, I forgot to ask you if you wanted Mexican or Anglo food."

"Do you have Italian?"

She laughed, trying to imitate an Italian accent. "*I'va gotta yoohoosa ana coco puffsa...*"

They laughed at having to speak so artificially even using movie dialogue. Martin coughed. "I'll meet you at the car in twenty minutes. We've got duds to buy and cowboy boots. And I want to stop at a computer store and buy a new iPad. Do I need a hat?"

"What? And flatten that blow-dried two hundred dollar haircut?"

The screen-protected clock on the wall of Las Flores' three-cell jailhouse indicated ten o'clock when Beryl and Martin Mazzavini, who was resplendent in shiny new jeans and a seventeen hundred dollar pair of python cowboy boots, entered the office. A uniformed man sat at the only desk, leaning back in his chair, staring out the window. Even when Martin closed the door and walked to the desk, the man did not turn to acknowledge him. "I'm Martin Mazzavini, Mr. Chang's attorney," Martin said to the back of his head. "I'd like to confer with my client."

The man swiveled his chair around. A 'deputy sheriff' star was pinned above one pocket and his name tag, *Peterson*, was pinned above the other. He unclasped hands that had been locked behind his head, and looked with some amusement at the visitor who was garbed in fresh out-of-the-box western raiment. "You're Chin's lawyer?" he asked as he stood halfway up to view Martin's boots. "Got any I.D.?" he asked in such a way that Beryl could tell he was insulting the Armani in Martin Mazzavini.

"Give him a little of that Wal-Mart catwalk," Beryl said as Martin furiously dug at the card slots in his wallet, trying to extract his laminated credentials.

Deputy Peterson said, *en passant*, "Nice boots."

"Personally," said Beryl, "I think a few accessories are needed. To complete the *ensemble*, a bolo tie with one of those Lucite-encased scorpions is absolutely *de rigueur*. What do you think, Deputy Peterson?"

"Yeah... that would work," he said. "Maybe you could find one in the souvenir shop at the fillin' station and be back in time for visiting hours."

"Oh," Beryl said apologetically as she got out her iPhone, "You weren't expecting us! The District Attorney's office in Tucson must have screwed up the appointment. They were supposed to notify you that we were here to consult with Adam Chang a.k.a. Aaron Chin. Let me call them and straighten this out." She had been pretending that their presence should have been announced. She was astonished to learn that it had been.

"No, no," the deputy said, standing up and taking a ring of keys off the wall. Miss Williams' office did call. I was just funnin' with ya'." He led them to Adam's cell and unlocked the door just as Martin finally succeeded in freeing his laminated cards. He thrust them at the deputy who pushed his hand away. "I believe you. I believe you. I mean, it ain't the kind of thing a man would lie about." He pushed the door open and let them enter the cell. "Holler when you're ready to come out," he said as he locked the door behind them.

Now Martin struggled to get the cards back into his wallet. "Remind me to get a new goddamned wallet!" he hissed at Beryl. He took a deep breath.

"Remind me to find out why anybody from the D.A.'s office called here. You don't need their permission, do you?"

"No. No, I don't." He took his new spiral tablet from his shirt pocket and wrote, "da cld las f jl.7/10. Y?"

Adam Chang was lying on his bed. Beryl could see a halo of wetness on his pillow. His clothes were fresh. She instinctively looked under the bed and saw numerous dead roaches on the floor. It puzzled her that so many of them appeared to have been squashed. "Adam!" she called, but though his eyes were open, he did not turn his head to look at her.

"Why are there squashed roaches under your bed?" She purposely asked him something that he had not prepared himself to ignore.

"They crawl on you at night. If you slap them fast, you can kill them. Then in the morning I just kick them under the bed. We could use a few bats in here. The bats would eat them, unless they've been poisoned. If the bats smell that poison, they won't eat them."

Beryl looked at Martin and they exchanged a look of alarm at Adam's oddly detached response. She pulled on Adam's shirt sleeve. "Sit up. Keep your voice low. We have good news."

He looked up at her. "Who are you?"

Beryl put a finger to her lips, indicating that he should speak softly. "My name's Beryl Tilson. I'm a P.I. Your father hired me. I'm working *pro bono*, repaying a favor. We've got a lot of new evidence and very little time to prepare it for presentation in court. So get up and answer the questions Mr. Mazzavini and I need to ask you."

Adam Chang sighed and swung his legs over the side of the bed. "What new evidence?"

Beryl whispered. "We're certain we can prove the murder weapon was planted and that the video recording is a fake."

Adam looked at Martin Mazzavini. "Is that true?"

"Of course. What the hell do you think we came here for? The local color?"

"He's mad at his wallet," Beryl explained.

Adam muttered, "What do you want to know?"

Beryl questioned him. "Somebody had to know you were messing around with the plants up here. When did you first get onto the Montoya land?"

"Recently or when I first saw it... that was when I was in my senior year."

"The time you were arrested."

"I came first on Friday, July 2nd."

"What time did you arrive and how long did you stay?"

"I stayed in Tucson and drove down after breakfast... so I usually arrived around noon."

"Usually? What other days did you come?"

"Everyday until I got arrested."

"Always at the same time?"

"Yeah. I drove down from Tucson."

"What did you see on July 5th?"

"I came down the road as usual. I was gonna park and walk up the mountain to sample more of the agave that grew at the highest elevation. Gross inspection by binoculars indicated a difference in color and size. It would have been my last sampling before I headed up to Nevada to meet my partners. I have partners."

"Ivan and Enrique?"

"Yes. You know them?"

"I talked to Enrique on the phone. He and Ivan told Harrison Metcalf they intend to testify for you."

"Mr. Metcalf didn't tell me that."

"We'll look into that. But continue with what happened when you got to the Montoya land."

"I saw a truck and another car... it was a red truck and a silver car... parked near where I usually park. I like to park in this one place because I can turn around and because there are a couple of trails that go to different parts. I saw them parked there and wondered what they were doing there - the red truck and the silver car."

"Yes, go on."

"There were men standing in front of the truck. I had to keep my eyes on the road. There are a lot of little ditches, ruts, in it. I heard shots. Four I think. So I hit the brakes and there was a small area right where I was that I could turn around in. I waited for a minute because I wasn't sure what had happened... whether it would change my plan to go up to the top. And then I saw only two men. There were more before. I decided to leave. I didn't know what was happening but I figured it wasn't good. So I turned around and started to drive back to the main road. I can't drive fast. My car is new, well, not new, just new for me. And I couldn't drive fast because of the ditches. The next thing I knew a helicopter is telling me to stop. I had some hash in the car and I panicked. It's funny that I remembered that I still hadn't registered the car... I had been a little short of funds... so I figured I'd just tell them I had been robbed of my identification. We were so close to the Mexican border and people had warned me about getting my I.D. stolen."

Martin asked, "Do you remember what else was in the trash bag and also what else was in your wallet?" He made a cryptic note about checking out the red truck and silver car. (ck rd trk & slv cr. tgs?)

"I had only one credit card. Mr. Metcalf had my account cancelled for me. Some photos, banana skins, chewing gum, used wet wipes and tissues, maybe a half dozen little hash bricks in those yellow 'Turksmoke' wrappers, gas receipts, my driver's license and cellphone. I knew I was coming to a bare patch of sand and that I'd be kicking up dust there if I turned sharply. So I kicked up a lot of dust and tossed the bag out the window. I was close to the main road and I figured that if I got away clean, I'd come back and retrieve my stuff. I left all my testing equipment in the car. I kept going, but the silver car came up behind me and a deputy ordered me to stop and get out of the car and made me lie on the ground. I can hear him looking through my car and then a police car came down the main road and stopped at the exit, the place I would have exited if I had gotten to the main road first. And then I was read my Miranda rights and cuffed and put in the police car. They said I shot two guys. I said that I didn't have a gun and they could test my hands for gunshot residue. I've seen enough crime shows to know about GSR. That's all I know."

"Did they ever test you?"

"No."

Martin shook his head and rubbed his eyes, trying to imagine how a client of his could be so mistreated. "I can't believe this! The guys who did the killing were the ones who pursued and arrested my client!"

"I told them to test my hands," Adam pleaded, apologetically. "I really did." Then he sighed and a cloud seemed to pass in front of his eyes.

Beryl wanted to question him before he fell asleep sitting up. "How do you know Ivan and Enrique?"

"I met them at a science fair in Raleigh, North Carolina. We just got to talking, and I told them about the invention I was working on."

"Your father said that you sent your biosphere cover letters to a friend who forwarded them to him. Who was that friend?"

Adam was reluctant to respond. "I've kept her out of it up to now. Why is it necessary to bring her into this? I don't want to complicate her life. She's a married lady."

"Suppose you cut the chivalry crap and answer the question. Who is she?" Beryl shook his shoulder. "Neither of us is being paid to be here. We can't help you if you won't help yourself."

"Jeez. Cool it. I don't think she'll like this. Her name is Sonya Lee. She lives in Tucson. At least she used to live there. I haven't seen her in a while... since Christmas. It was before Christmas."

"Where does she live?"

"Lorean Apartments." Then, as if to prove that she existed, he whispered in a childlike voice, "Here, I can show you a letter from her." He removed from his boot a plastic bag that contained half a dozen letters. He opened the bag and handed Beryl an envelope.

The handwriting on the expensive rag bond paper was meticulously scripted. It had been written in old-fashioned ink and not a ballpoint pen. Beryl and Martin stared at the envelope, admiring it. Then Beryl took note of the postmark. "Is this the last letter you received from Sonya Lee? It was mailed to you in January."

"January? Let me see that." Adam reached for the envelope. "Yes," he said, "it does say January."

Beryl remembered the street address and wrote it in her small tablet. Martin copied her note into his tablet.

"How many letters do you have from her?" Beryl asked as she gently took Sonya Lee's letter from Adam's hands. "I'll see to it that you get this back," she said, tucking it into her tote bag.

"I had a bunch of them, but they started disappearing every time I got moved. I liked some lines she wrote in that letter. She's so talented.

I kept that envelope aside." He looked through the remaining envelopes in the bag. "This is all official stuff, I guess."

"Let me see," Martin said, reaching for the remaining envelopes. He opened them. "This one is from Metcalf. He's going on annual leave and suggests you contact another member of his 'team.' Fortunately," he shook his head and laughed, "that let's me out." He looked at the remaining letters. "And these advise Adam about no bail and about court dates. And that's all there is?"

"That's all I know of." Adam's eyes closed.

"What happened to all your scientific notes and specimens?" Beryl asked.

"Maybe they're in the lost and found in the motel in Tucson. I didn't get a chance to get any specimens on the last day. Everything else was in my room in Tucson. Room #14, the "Dew-Drop-Inn" on Oracle Road. I don't know where the stuff is that was in my car. I don't know where my car is, either."

"We'll check it out." She felt his cheek and turned to Martin. "He's got a fever, I think. Tell me straight. Don't exaggerate. Does your grandfather have any real muscle? Any markers to call in, connections, drag, that is, beyond your boyhood's charming tendency to idolize him?"

"You're asking me? He doesn't get parking tickets fixed. But he gets things done."

"Will he get involved as a favor to you?"

"More as a favor to Adam. My grandfather went to Duke. They have some holy alliance that nobody discusses. But yes, as a favor to me, too."

"Then let's get your grandfather involved in the care and feeding of this prisoner. This filth and Adam's obvious malnutrition and illness have got to end immediately. If your grandfather has the right connections he can have this boy transferred up to a decent facility in Tucson."

Adam looked up at them. "I have a bad toothache too. The last time, or maybe the time before, I'm not sure, they put a drunken guy in here who hit me and knocked a tooth loose. I asked them for a dentist, but I never got one. Some nights it hurts so bad I can't sleep."

Martin stooped down and then knelt until he was face-to-face with Adam. He whispered, "They knew we were coming today. Is that why you got a shower and clean clothes?"

"I guess so. They didn't tell me you were coming."

"I see that your jaw is swollen. When did you last have a shower and clean clothes?"

"I don't know. Last week maybe. I don't know. Two weeks ago?"

"Listen, Adam. Stay quiet. Don't talk to anyone. No one. I am going to see to it that you get proper care immediately and that very shortly you will get your freedom. Do you understand?"

"Yes. Can I lay back down now? I'm a little tired."

"Adam, before this day is over, you are going to see a dentist and get some medical treatment and good food. I swear this to you." He looked up at Beryl. "Call Deputy Peterson. We're through for now."

When Deputy Peterson unlocked the cell door Beryl asked him how they could get to Nubes Road. He thought for a moment. "Wayne McPeak's place? Just go back as if you're headin' to Tucson, by the way you came. After you turn on Sasabe, about two miles down you'll see an old Indian style house... you know with the tree beams sticking through the adobe... tan color. That's Wayne McPeak's place."

Outside in the parking lot, Martin stopped before they got into the car. "Let's hear how poetic Miss Sonya Lee is. He got out his tablet as Beryl removed the letter from her bag. She leaned against the car and read aloud:

My Darling Adam, Omitofo!

I could not bear being away from you for the holidays. Everyone is so artificially happy. The solstice marks the advent of our Future Buddha... Christmas, indeed! They have commercialized what is truly sacred, our hope for the future.

In my sorrow, I flew to Vancouver, to my parents' home. Alone, I walked until there were only natural things to see. No... no... nothing man-made for me! Man-made are our sorrows! Man-made are the grievous circumstances that separate us. And then a terrible dread seized me and words formed in my mind, expressing the dread I felt about your problems. And all I could see from where I stood was three long mountains and a wood. So then I turned around, and when I looked the other way, I saw three islands in a bay. It began to rain and I thought of death and I could hear the drops strike my leather jacket. The rain must have a friendly sound to one who's six feet underground.

"Oh, my God!" Beryl announced with an exaggerated fury. "This is what is wrong with American education! A science and math major knows squat about literature! He thinks Sonya Lee writes beautifully. I guess. She's liberally quoting Edna St. Vincent Millay!"

"Who?" asked Martin innocently.

"I give up. 'Who?' This is what is wrong with American law students. They don't know squat about literature!"

"Edna who? I want to copy the name down correctly." He was obviously teasing.

Beryl wanted to laugh. Instead, she said calmly, "I may not be armed now; but I know karate and I will knock you on your Blue-Light Special Levi's."

"Hey! Blue-Light Specials are K-Mart, not Wal-Mart. *That* I know. My nanny used to take me all the time. Please continue with the epistle."

Beryl skimmed silently over the rest of the letter. "It's more of the same... plagiarism. At the end she says that she returned from Vancouver and tried even harder to raise money for a more professional defense for him... which despite her earlier feelings of dread, she is certain he will not require. She hopes to see him in February. She does not say what year that February will fall in."

"Please to get into the car, Beryl-san. You drive." Martin got into the passenger's seat. He looked at Sonya Lee's letter. "What does Omitofo mean? Is it some kind of code?"

"No. It's the way the Chinese say, Amitabha. The big Buddha... not Siddhartha."

"I believe you," he said, taking out his tablet and making cryptic notes. "Ind rep n gn disc. lb tm tst. tim tst trvl diam bl 2 flrs. cl rec Grca est tim." As Beryl turned onto Sasabe Road, Martin said, "I'm gonna break precedent and call my grandfather directly. Protocol demands that I call my dad first. He and my father are always arguing and I am always in the middle. So that became the rule. Dad first. But Dad didn't go to Duke. Don't ask. My family can be weird at times."

"I believe you," Beryl said. She pointed through the windshield. "Isn't that Wayne's house? The crime scene is across from it. Do me a favor and take the binoculars out of my tote bag. Just in case..."

The house, sitting back about a hundred feet from the road, was surprisingly well built and maintained. A paved sandstone walkway that was flanked by palo verde trees led to the front door. The entire facade of the house was open to the street, but the "porch" that McPeak testified to was actually an entryway alcove with tightly interlocked six inch diameter tree trunks or branches as its roof. The walkway's paved sandstones continued to become the floor and threshold. Against the alcove walls stood large brightly enameled Mexican pots that overflowed with blooming iceplants, sedum, myrtle and other succulents. The front door was a dark, heavy wooden door, carved in the Spanish style; but the wood trim around the windows was painted an unusual shade of muted aquamarine. Interior bamboo shades prevented anyone from seeing beyond the glass. Although the front was unprotected, flowering vines and stalks lay tangled on top of walls that extended from either side of the house. Large stick-slatted wrought iron gateways were built into the walls to block passage of two sandstone paved driveways that led to them from the road. "It's a rather nice place," Beryl said.

"More to the point," Martin added, "the owner - at least as he 'presents' himself - and the house do not match. They do not fit!" He made a note. "'Pork burritos on my front porch.' My ass! What do you call those red flowers that hang over the wall? They were also on the patio of our rooms."

"Bougainvillea. Pretty stuff. Do you want to drive onto the crime scene?"

"No... later, maybe. Right now I've got a client that needs help. Just park."

Martin called his grandfather. He spoke in an intimate, familial voice. "Pop Pop, I need to speak to you man-to-man. I need your help. And I need your help bad." There was a pause. "No, it's nothing like that. I'm in Arizona trying to save the life of a new client... a young scientist... a recent Duke graduate... a really decent American citizen who is being caged in filth, starved, he's feverish, he's got an infected tooth that was knocked loose when he was beaten by a violent drunk that they put inside his cell, and he is being given no - absolutely no - medical treatment, and he's clearly suffering from malnutrition after a year of this abuse. He is being railroaded in so many ways I can't begin to count them all."

Beryl shook her head. It was a perfect demonstration of exasperated pleading.

A firm note of reverence entered Martin's voice. "Pop Pop, I have no standing down here. I'm nobody. But you're somebody. You can move mountains. Justice and fairness mean something to you, and people know it, and they respect you for it. I need you to help this client not just because he's one of your fellow Duke alumni or because it's my first capital case. Forget all that. I want you to help me to stand up for what is right! I need you, Pop Pop. Will you help me?" There was a pause. "No, nobody else. Who else can do what you can do?" Another pause. "Thank you, Pop Pop. This is what I've learned so far..."

Beryl smiled as she turned onto the highway to Tucson. The most junior Mazzavini carefully laid out the case to the most senior Mazzavini who apparently was writing down the corrections that had to be made, the tests that had to be run, the insurance payouts that had to be determined, and the many warrants that had to be obtained. The last request Martin had made was that all medical reports - laboratory test results and physician's evaluations - be copied in certified form at the request of Adam Chang and all necessary affidavits attesting to their validity be obtained. "These people are slick. We don't want any of the records altered in any way." It was a request to which the eldest Mazzavini replied, "Gotcha'."

"I'm so goddam hungry I could eat a pork burrito," Martin said as he swiped through his iPhone looking for a restaurant. He called ahead to a steakhouse and made reservations.

As they were pulling in to the parking lot, a medivac helicopter flew southwest over their heads. "Do you think?" Beryl asked.

Martin shrugged. "My grandfather loves Duke. He went there, both undergrad and law. My father insisted on going to Northwestern, both undergrad and law, and broke his heart. Anything, Lieutenant, is possible."

"How come you went to Cornell?"

"They fought so much when the time came for me to apply to college my mother got violent. I wound up going where her father went. Cornell. I also went to Cornell Law. *And if you had to choose between me and my father...*"

"*I'd choose you any day of the week and twice on Sundays.*"

As they finished lunch Beryl noted that it was past three o'clock. She took out her phone. "Let's see if Adam's in Las Flores." She called the jail.

Deputy Peterson was still on duty. "Some people came with a court order and took him away," he said. "Medical people."

"Did they tell you where they were taking him?"

"No. And I didn't ask. But he's gone. A judge in Tucson signed the order. I didn't get his name."

Beryl put her phone away. "Well, Martin, what would you like to do next?" she asked.

"Whatever it is that my grandfather can't handle from his office. Let's call on Miss Sonya Lee. I say 'Miss' because I somehow doubt that she's anybody's missus."

The Lorean apartments, a two-storey pinkish-tan stucco box decorated with palm trees and surrounded by a pinkish-tan pebbled lawn decorated with patches of lantana, promised little in the way of exotic adventure. There were four stairways, one at each corner, marked by the wall's indicator: A, B, C, and D. Sonya Lee's apartment was on the D side of the square building. They climbed the stairs and went to her apartment, #218, and knocked on the door.

A middle-aged oriental housekeeper whose hair was pulled straight back and knotted tightly at the nape of her neck, stood imperiously in the doorway. She wore silk, a long black fitted dress with side slits and a row of frogs that terminated at a high mandarin collar. Martin gulped, swallowing down the authoritative words he had planned to use. Beryl was not so easily intimidated. "We're here to see Miss Lee." She produced a business card and extended it to the woman who did not reach for it. As if it were a playing card, Beryl curved the card and flipped it past the woman into the room. "Perhaps," she said to Martin in an obviously contrived benign voice, "she cannot read." Again, in a voice that was nearly a shout, she said, "Miss Lee! We are here to see Miss Lee!"

From inside the apartment came a sweet voice. "Wang Tai Tai, is someone calling for me?"

The woman picked up the business card and read it with a Chinese accent. "Some private investigators from Philadelphia."

Martin extended his card. "I am Martin Mazzavini, from Chicago. I'm Mr. Adam Chang's attorney."

The woman amended her announcement. "One say he is Adam Chang's attorney."

"Let them in," said the voice that had a slight British accent.

Beryl, whose taste in furniture confined itself to Japanese Zen, winced to see the raucous enameled black, gold, and red over-decorated Chinese furniture, off-center thick piled medallion rugs, fringed lampshades with ceramic figurine bases and calligraphic scrolls hanging everywhere.

Sonya Lee lay like a nearly Naked Maja on a chaise longue in a bay window at the far end of the apartment. A window was open and a breeze blew a censer's cloud of incense smoke across her body. She was beautiful and, in a diaphanous negligée, impossible to look away from. Beryl and Martin walked back to her wondering if she were some kind of invalid. They could see through the glass behind her that the rear of the apartments all opened onto a central, luxuriantly landscaped courtyard. A fountain gurgled at its center.

"I am Sonya Lee," Miss Lee said softly as she extended her right hand to Martin, positioning her fingers just a few inches above her dark left nipple. Beryl wondered whether she wanted Martin to kiss her hand or possibly her lightly covered nipple. Martin bowed and gently took her fingers into his. He simply murmured, "Martin Mazzavini, at your service."

Beryl cleared her throat. "We'd like to ask you a few questions about Adam Chang."

"Such a dear boy," Miss Lee semi-whined. "Such a pity he got himself involved with those awful people. I hope his second trial will go well. I'm sure the Court will show him leniency because of his age. What did you want to ask me?"

"How long have you known Adam?" Martin asked.

"Let me think... I met him in the spring of 2008. Yes... I had planned to go to Mardi Gras in Rio de Janeiro, but Easter fell so early that year... on March 22nd or 23rd... and forty days before that would have meant that Ash Wednesday fell early in February. It was much too close to Christmas and New Year's, not to mention the lunar New Year. The holidays do tend to tire me out."

"Where did you meet him?" Beryl asked.

"Here in Tucson... or perhaps a little south of here. I have friends who have delightful haciendas near the border."

"I would have thought that - since you became such pen-pals - you'd be able to recall more precisely the circumstances of the meeting."

"Pen-pals? I don't understand your use of the term. A few letters of encouragement to a lonely boy of Chinese descent hardly made me his pen-pal."

"May I inquire," Martin said, "about the last time you communicated with him?"

"I sent him a Christmas card. Even Buddhists wish others to be of good cheer during the holidays."

"So your relationship was platonic?" Martin asked.

"My dear Mr. Mazzavini, it hardly qualified as even platonic. I was acquainted with the boy. We had no relationship. Now, if there is nothing more?"

Beryl looked out the window. "What a wonderful view you have out your window. I have no view from my window. But where I used to live, all I could see from where I stood was three long mountains and a wood. Enchanting. Mr. Mazzavini has a few more questions to ask you, personal ones, I think. So if you'll excuse me, I'll go and wait while he conducts his personal inquiry." She turned and walked out of the apartment, unimpeded by a door, since Wang Tai Tai stood erect, holding the front door open.

Beryl immediately descended the stairs and opened a gate that led back into the courtyard. As she walked back to the rear, she took a newly purchased digital cellular phone scanner/recorder from her tote bag. She stood under Sonya Lee's window and without listening to it, recorded the call Sonya made the moment Martin left.

Martin did not at first understand why Beryl had quoted Sonya's letter, obviously tipping her off that she had read the letter Adam received. He also did not know what personal questions he was supposed to ask. He therefore did his best to appear pleasant and asked her such "personal" questions as: Did she go to Brazil often? Did she like living in the Southwest? Was she a vegetarian Buddhist? What kind of incense was currently being used? Finally, having exhausted his repertoire of personal questions, he thanked her for her cooperation and left. Wang Tai Tai held the door open for him, too.

When he saw Beryl under Sonya's windows he walked more softly and said nothing. He stood beside her watching the recording indicator light. When it went out, she raised her index finger telling him to wait to see if Sonya would make another call. She did. Martin noticed that someone across the courtyard was watching them. He whispered this to Beryl and then put his arms around her and acted amorously. The person who had been watching turned away.

When the second call ended, Beryl waited another minute, pretending to be speaking to Martin. He pretended to answer. When no cellphone call was made, they turned and left. When they got to the Lorean's parking lot, they discovered that all four of their car's tires had been slashed.

Beryl immediately called the car rental agency. They agreed to send a maintenance man with four new tires. While they waited Beryl called Sensei Percy Wong in Philadelphia.

Sensei occupied a two-storey storefront building half a block away from Wagner & Tilson Private Investigators' office. The ground floor of the building functioned as a small Zen Buddhist temple with a kitchenette in the rear. He lived on the second floor which is where he was when her call came in. He was preparing for bed.

"What's up?" he asked."

"I'll be brief. I'm in Tucson. Last night my hotel room was ransacked. Today the car I rented had its tires slashed. I'm in the beginning of a murder and drug trafficking case. I'm with a young lawyer from Chicago, Martin Mazzavini. He and I are in the same dangerous boat. Can you come out here?"

"How's tomorrow? Tonight I'll arrange for someone to relieve me at the dojo and the temple. Does George know?"

"He knows I'm here; but he doesn't know about the dangers. I can't ask him to come because we might be climbing up and down some desert hills. His knee couldn't take it. And there's also a Chinese connection. Do me a favor and call him to let him know you're coming; but don't tell him that I wanted you here because I'm worried. Make something up. Then call me back with your flight information."

"I'll call you back and you can pick me up at the airport."

The man was still changing the tires when Beryl indicated to Martin that they walk to the end of the block where a small dog park began. They sat down on the pavement and leaned against a wall. Beryl took the scanner from her tote back and got out her tablet.

"I want it stated for the record," Martin stated firmly, "that I had nothing to do with the purchase of any illegal eavesdropping or recording equipment, or with the information gained from using such illegally gathered material. I did not make the recordings and I will not listen to them. Do you understand?"

"Yes," she said. "I have been so notified." The equipment had been in the bag the store used when she purchased it. The receipt for $238.71 was in the bag. She pulled it out and showed it to him.

He whistled, "Primo. Nice choice."

"It does everything," Beryl said. She returned the receipt to the bag and put the recorder's earpiece into her ear and turned on the equipment. On her tablet she wrote, "2 Wayne: 2 R snoopng. Is nxt shpmnt n jeprdy?" Ans: "No. Don't panic. Harley knows. All controlled.

"2nd 2 Hugo: Keep eye on Wayne. 2 R snooping. He may be weak link. Ans: W knows what he's doing. The trial wl b ovr soon."

She wrote, 'Sonya & W & H & Harley?' Beryl closed the tablet and shut off the recorder.

"Holy shit!" Martin exclaimed. "We have the witness, the deputy, and now the girlfriend, plus whoever the hell Harley is! And they're all arrayed against him. Jesus. Adam has been a marked man in this whole operation. Everything in the scenario depends on his being the fall guy at least in this particular drug trafficking incident. We suspected that this was a set up, but I don't think that even you expected it to be so elaborately constructed.

As they returned to the Arroyo Motel, Martin wrote on his tablet, "Let's go out for the evening and check into another motel. We need to take one of the cars back to the rental and maybe get another one."

He handed the tablet to Beryl who scrawled an answer: "We'll have to leave our clothing behind."

Martin bent over and whispered in her ear, "I'll change for dinner." Then he bent his face farther forward so that she could whisper in his ear, "Wear those python boots with that dark blue Armani."

Aloud, for the benefit of those who possibly were listening, he said clearly, "Say, I'd like to take a few souvenirs back with me. Stop in one of those shops so that I can get a couple of bolo ties, you know, the kind with scorpions. My grandfather loves opera. He really likes Puccini's stuff. That *Tosca* has a guy named Scorpio he always sings along with. It's a deeper voice."

"I don't speak Italian so I can't tell you what the guy's name means, but it isn't Scorpio it's *Scarpia*."

He mouthed the words, "I know!" Aloud, he said in what he called a "Lakeshore Redneck" dialect, "Scorpio, *Scarpia*. What's the goddamn difference."

They soon passed a roadside mall that featured a souvenir shop. Beryl pulled into the parking lot.

They returned one car and exchanged the other for a new "alarmed" SUV and then checked into a motel. They obtained a double room on the ground floor and were able to park directly in front of their room. Beryl left the drape open so that, with no light on in the room, they were able to observe any activity around the car.

As they were settling into the new room, Martin's grandfather called. Martin put the phone on speaker. "Nits!" Massimiliano Mazzavini roared. "That young man had cooties! Oh, they were sure to wash his hair before you got there, but they didn't use one of those nit combs and the doctors had to have a nurse spend an hour combing it. They wanted to shave his head, but I said, 'No! That boy has to be ready for trial!' I was so upset that the Governor had to calm me down. She didn't want to hear a Chicago Republican weep. Told me it would be unseemly. Told me to trust her. You tell that Blue Devil that I have got his back."

They decided they would bathe, dress for dinner, and go out without feeling like actors in a Cold War drama.

At seven o'clock Martin put one of his new bolo ties on and said, "Let's go out and get that dinner! How do you like Scorpion a la Armani?"

Beryl looked at him. "I would not go to a McDonald's drive thru with you wearing that thing around your neck. There are brujas around here that can make that creature come alive and start crawling up your throat."

"*Nobody likes you very much,*" he said, feigning insult to his sartorial judgment.

After dinner, they stopped at another western clothing and farm supply store and bought more shirts, jeans, socks, and a large insulated picnic cooler.

SATURDAY, JUNE 11, 2011.

They slept late and instead of breakfast, they had an early lunch. Neither had realized how exhausting Friday had been.

Martin called ahead to the District Attorney's office. His call was forwarded to ADA Williams who had prosecuted the original case and who would be prosecuting the retrial. Martin introduced himself and stated his purpose. "I want to examine some of the evidence from the Aaron Chin a.k.a. Adam Chang case."

"I'm afraid you're too late," she said. "A federal marshal just took custody of the evidence about twenty minutes ago. A civil rights violation has been filed against this office." She gave him the marshal's name and phone number.

Martin thanked her and turned to Beryl. "The feds are stealing or protecting the evidence. Maybe we'll get lucky." He called the number he had been given and left a voicemail message stating that he wanted to inspect the evidence they were holding.

Beryl smiled at the news. "That would have mattered more before, when we didn't know what to believe. But now, knowing whether hands were raised when the shot was fired, isn't so important. After we pick Sensei up at the airport, let's go down and look at the crime scene."

They left the motel, put the records and tote bag into the cooler, and went to pick Sensei up. Martin waited in the car while Beryl went in to meet Sensei's flight.

In their "new" rental car, Beryl drove and Martin sat in the passenger's seat. Sensei tossed his carry-on bag into the back of the SUV and sat in the seat behind Beryl.

Free finally to speak without restraint, they discussed the case as they drove down to the Montoya land.

As they neared Wayne McPeak's house, Martin pulled over and directed Sensei's attention to the building. "The guy who owns this is one of the two principal witnesses against Adam Chang. I figure him for the brains of the outfit. He testified like an idiot, but it was all perjured testimony. Very clever stuff."

Beryl advised, "Nice place. Get a good look. We'll be turning onto the desert in just a moment." She slowed down and turned onto a dirt road and proceeded slowly.

Sensei remembered that he was still wearing canvas topped lightweight tennis shoes. "I'll get my hiking boots out of my bag. Cloth shoes aren't the best thing to wear walking through cactus." He turned and began to belly-slide over the seat back. A bullet pierced the window behind Beryl just as Sensei dropped to the floor. It exited the window behind Martin, leaving a webbed hole in both panes of glass.

"Jesus!" Martin shouted. "Get down."

"What the hell are they doing! Aiming at me?" Sensei frantically whispered as Martin and Beryl crouched down in the front seats. "That bullet would have gone right through me!"

Beryl stopped the car. For more than a minute there was nothing but silence. She whispered to Martin, "Let's do that movie thing. Take the brim of your hat, like this," she held the edge of her hat, "and slowly elevate your hat as I lift mine up. We'll fake heads."

The two hats seemed cautiously to rise above the front seat. Immediately another bullet pierced her side window, penetrated the hats, and exited Martin's window. "That shot would have destroyed a perfectly good lawyer," she said.

"Is this the time for humor?" Martin hissed, and then, hearing a voice outside, whispered, "Quiet!"

"Don't shoot the windshield!" It was the voice they had heard on the reporter's video, the angry voice of Wayne McPeak. "We've gotta drive the car outta here and we don't need the attention of a bullet ridden windshield!"

"Lemme' see if I got 'em," Garcia called. "Cover me."

Sensei flattened his body against the rear of the back seat, concealing himself as much as possible.

The door slowly began to open on Beryl's side. As soon as the opening was about six inches wide, Beryl pushed the door, knocking Garcia off balance. He staggered back as she sprang against his legs, butting her forehead against his diaphragm. The rifle he carried fired harmlessly into the air. McPeak, on the other side of the vehicle, could not shoot for fear of hitting Garcia.

"Hold it!" McPeak shouted. "Hold it or he gets it!" Beryl looked back. The passenger door was open and a gun was pointed at Martin's head.

Garcia struck Beryl's head with the rifle's stock, sending her to the ground, dazed.

'Get outta the car!" McPeak commanded. Martin unfolded himself to get his feet down onto the ground. "Bring 'er!" McPeak shouted. "Let's get 'em back away from the road. Got zips on ya'?"

"Yeah," Garcia called, stepping on Beryl's hand as he pulled a plastic zip tie from his pocket. He inserted her wrists into the loops and tightened the strap. Grabbing a fistful of her hair, he began to drag her away from the car. She said nothing, pretending to be unconscious. She kept repeating to herself, as a mantra, "Thank God, Sensei is here."

Martin stumbled forward. McPeak called, "Put cuffs on him, too."

Garcia dropped Beryl, letting her fall against the edge of a cholla cactus. He shouted at Martin, "Put your hands behind ya', asshole!" As McPeak stood there pointing a weapon at him, Martin did as he was told, and a zip tie was tightened around his wrists. Garcia again grabbed Beryl's hair and dragged her a hundred feet to a dry wash in which a pickup truck was parked.

Garcia dumped Beryl on the ground behind the truck. McPeak slipped on a leather glove and lowered the tailgate. "Toss her in here! And you," he said to Martin, "climb in and lay down. As Martin lifted his thigh onto the tailgate he could feel the searing heat of the metal. He did not give any indication of pain.

Garcia picked Beryl up by the hair and her waist belt and unceremoniously tossed her onto the grooved truck bed. "Where are we taking them?" he called.

McPeak opened the pickup's door on the driver's side. "Let's think this through. This place is gonna be crawling with those forensic people tomorrow, doin' tests. I don't want these assholes killed here. We can take them to my place and put them in the wine cellar. But we have to get them out by dinnertime. Where's the nearest mine shaft?"

"Green Valley, in one of the copper mines."

"Ok. We'll hold 'em in my place and as soon as the sun goes down we'll take them up there and dump them. You drive their car back to that old barn on Nubes."

McPeak climbed into the driver's side of the truck. Garcia got into the passenger's seat.

The side of the truck bed that Beryl was on had been partially in shade; but Martin's side was sizzling in the sun. He was on his belly and already he could feel the metal snap buttons of his western shirt burning his flesh. "Wiggle your head over here," Beryl whispered, surprising him since he had thought she was unconscious. "Put your face on my hair!" She turned her face away from him and flipped her hair back as far as she could. Her hair was only shoulder length but it was enough to give him some protection against the metal.

Martin buried his nose against her collar. "Jesus," he kept repeating, "this is like hell. Jesus, I'm burnin' up."

In her mind Beryl kept thinking about the dark coolness of the wine cellar and the dark coolness of the mine shaft. They began to seem inviting. Sensei will act, she told herself.

The pick-up truck bounced along the uneven desert trail, causing Beryl and Martin to roll and slide in the truck bed. With their hands tied behind them, they had no way to steady themselves and flopped painfully against the hot metal ridges of the floor. Finally the truck stopped beside their SUV. Garcia got out, carrying his rifle.

McPeak lowered his window and called, "Lower the side windows so that the holes don't show."

Garcia went to the SUV and got in the driver's side. He expected the keys to be in the ignition, but they were not. He got out and slammed the door shut and walked around to the passenger's side. He searched on the seat and under it. He found nothing. "Where the hell are the keys?" he yelled.

"They have to be in there!" McPeak answered angrily. "Open your eyes!"

Garcia returned to the driver's side and got into the car and felt around the floor under the seat. "I'm telling you there are no keys in here!" He got out of the SUV and gestured to McPeak, "Look for yourself!"

McPeak turned off the ignition and got out of the pickup. "Where the hell can they be? Did you look under the seat... or maybe they got kicked out."

Sensei waited until both men were together on the ground. He wanted them to be close to each other. As Garcia stepped back from the opened door so that McPeak could get into the driver's seat, Sensei shot out from behind the SUV, kicked Garcia in the chest and grabbed McPeak's right arm, pulled and twisted it, forcing him downwards, and with a *Ippontsuki* one knuckle fist strike to the base of his skull, he felled McPeak who collapsed onto the ground. Immediately he brought his right hand up in the *shuto uchi* knifeblade hand and struck the gasping Garcia in the throat. He gathered their weapons and went to the truck bed.

He vaulted over the tailgate and immediately went to Beryl. "These are new zip restraints. You'll have to be patient." He lowered the tailgate and pulled his two companions out.

As they returned to the SUV, Martin cursed the two men who were lying on the ground. "Let's make sure they don't get up!" He balanced himself, preparing to kick McPeak's head.

"No!" Beryl shouted. "They're dead! Don't put your boot print on them."

Martin did not believe it. He turned to Sensei. "What does she mean, 'they're dead'?"

"Because," Sensei said gently, "one has his windpipe broken and the other has his neck broken at the base of his skull. They have already taken their last breath of air on this good earth. Incidentally, I don't have a knife."

"My binoculars are in the cooler," Beryl said. Martin's eyes showed that he did not understand anything and that it was wiser not to speak.

Sensei opened the cooler, got out the binoculars and dislodged a lens. Since Beryl was wearing cowboy boots and could not "step-through" her hands to bring them in front of her, she held her hands behind her. Sensei put a protective "pot holder" shirt on the hood's metal and positioned her hands on top of the shirt. Then he held the lens so that the focal point of light that passed through it shown on the nylon knot. Smoke immediately lifted from the connection as the concentrated beam drilled a hole through the plastic. In less than five minutes, Beryl was completely free. "Your turn, Counselor," she said, shaking her hands to improve the blood's circulation. "And whatever you do, don't move your hands while Sensei's working on the plastic."

Martin stood where she had been standing and placed his hands up behind him, offering no resistance to Sensei's manipulations. "I've got to get out of the house more," he said, thinking aloud.

They called the real sheriff's office in Sasabe and, after stuffing socks into the bullet holes of the SUV's windows, Sensei produced the keys, started the car, and turned up the air conditioning. Within the hour, a deputy sheriff and the coroner arrived, took statements, and bagged the dead men.

"I need to get some medical treatment," Martin complained. The deputy looked at his ear and agreed. "Do you want me to call a medivac helicopter?"

"No," Martin declined. "I just want to get back to the motel and get under a cold shower. I'll stop at an emergency room and get the burns looked at." He gave him his business card and wrote the Arroyo's name and phone number on the back along with his private cellphone line.

"I need to get some medical treatment, too," Beryl said. "My skin isn't as bad as Martin's, but it does hurt, and I have a few cholla barbs to get taken out. Incidentally, Sensei will be staying with me at the Arroyo. I need to get under cold water, too. Take pictures of our wrists and burns, and let us get on our way."

The coroner's assistant took official photos, and Beryl, Sensei and Martin took more photographs with their iPhones. Beryl told Martin to take off his shirt, and in his windy-city pallor, the burns received from the truck bed showed themselves as pink stripes and circular buttons.

Martin was still troubled by the court's acceptance of "video evidence" of the gun's discovery. "How the hell did that get put in front of a jury? Why didn't anybody see it?"

"Not everybody is looking with a detective's eye," Beryl replied. "We know that a terrible crime has been committed and we believe in our government. The video was a drama, and a drama requires us to suspend credulity. We see the dragon breathe fire and we casually believe it. The gun is searched for and found. There was no break in the film sequence. It's accepted.

"When a jury's handled properly, it becomes an audience of twelve, not twelve independent judges, but an audience ready to suspend credulity. Individually and outside the legal theater, each one of them might have said, 'No way!' but they weren't individuals and they really weren't thinking. They were watching a show."

Sensei drove the SUV directly to a hospital emergency room in Tucson. As they waited, Beryl inquired at the reception desk if Adam Chang had been admitted there. The receptionist checked and said that they should try another hospital.

Martin's burns were treated with silver sulfadiazine. His ear was bandaged. Both he and Beryl received a prescription for pain and a small tube of burn medication. While Martin was still sitting in the treatment room, the doctor suggested that Sensei purchase a white "scrub suit" type of shirt and pants in the gift shop for Martin to wear as further protection against infection for the few areas that had begun to blister.

They left for the drug store to get the prescription filled, and then, finally, they entered the lobby of the Arroyo Motel.

Beryl was prepared to insist that they be given their original rooms and that her room should be considered a double room. Fortunately, no insistence was necessary: the rooms were available and rather than a cot, the clerk had a twin bed assembled and dressed in Martin's room.

Sensei helped Martin into his bedroom. "Don't sit on the bedspread," he warned. "They usually don't clean them with any sort of regularity." He pulled the spread down and folded it at the bottom of the bed.

"Yes," said Beryl. "We had a case not too long ago in which a woman claimed to have been raped on a motel bed with the spread still covering it... and when the spread was analyzed for DNA, they found 32 different semen samples on it. Stay away from bedspreads. The sheets are fine."

Martin's eyes rolled helplessly. "What an education I'm getting." He had taken one of his pain pills and was struggling to stay awake. "I want to call my grandfather to bring him up to date."

"Then do so immediately," Sensei said. "You're having a tough time keeping your eyes open. If you reach him, tell him immediately that you may fall asleep so he doesn't worry. I'll shut the door between the rooms to give you some privacy. I'll look in on you in fifteen minutes. Is that all right?"

Martin agreed and Sensei closed the door. "Now," he said to Beryl, "tell me everything that's going on."

"It's clear that one of our biggest problems is the relationship between Sonya Lee and the two killers, McPeak and Garcia. And who is Harley? And also, Ivan and Enrique haven't acted in a way that puts them above suspicion. I don't know how they're involved, but something's wrong with those two. Martin's grandfather is tracking down their partnership agreement. You know that story: lure a sucker into business, take out big insurance policies on his presence in the 'organization,' frame or kill him and collect. Fix things so that you can claim the rights to assets he brought into the partnership - in his case, his filtration patent. The s.o.b.'s."

Sensei went into Martin's room and found him asleep with the phone still beside his left cheek. He turned the phone off and let him sleep. When he returned to Beryl's room he left the door open. Her eyes were beginning to close. He asked, "Where does Sonya Lee live?"

Beryl told him in a weakening voice and Sensei went into the bathroom, showered, shaved, and put on a Zen monk's tunic, knickers, and knee socks. He put on a cotton "street" robe and left the motel. He drove to the Lorean apartments.

Wang Tai Tai was appreciably more gracious. "Sifu," she said. "Welcome. She spoke Cantonese Chinese to him, and he explained that he did not speak any of the Chinese dialects. "It was my mother's wish that her children be raised purely American."

"I trust that you followed her into Buddhism," she said, bowing her head slightly.

"Of course," he replied. "Omitofo!'

She smiled. "Did you wish to call on Miss Lee?"

"Yes. Is she at home?"

"Yes, but she is not dressed to receive a priest... not in the Chinese tradition."

"I belong to a celibate order, of course," said Sensei. "But I am strong in my vows and leave the worry about temptation to younger monks."

"Very well. I will tell her that. Sifu? I'm afraid I don't know your name."

"Yao Feng. Shi Yao Feng."

"Please sit for a moment, Sifu. I'll tell Miss Lee you're here."

Sensei looked around the room and found it as distasteful as Beryl had found it. It was so incredibly cluttered, he thought. Unfortunately, Beryl had not prepared him for Miss Lee's uncommon beauty and when he was led back to her alcove, which was now illuminated with a dozen candles, he was stunned by her appearance.

"Sifu," Miss Lee cooed. "Come and sit beside me." The only chair available for him to sit on was placed so close to her chaise longue that his knees brushed against the long chair's upholstery.

"Did you know," she asked, "that not too long ago in the caves of Dun Huang they discovered sheet music used by the musicians who played at court during the Tang dynasty? It was necessary to find or to reconstruct some of the ancient instruments, but the government succeeded in doing that and then the national orchestra recorded the compositions. Would you like to hear an arrangement made by a friend of mine? The music is authentic, I assure you."

"Yes, I'd like that very much," Sensei replied. Miss Lee clicked on a Wave Radio on the other side of her long chair and immediately the haunting sound of strings being stroked and plucked in a mysterious oriental melody sounded. Sensei studied her face. It was, he thought, perfection.

Her negligée slipped from her leg and between being mesmerized by her pubic hair and dark nipples, exquisite face, incense, candle glow, and hypnotic music, he decided that whatever it was that had brought him to the Lorean apartments was no longer all that important.

"Am I correct in assuming you are here on behalf of Adam Chang?"

Sensei was relieved to be brought back into the present moment's awareness. "Yes, the case is rather bizarre."

"Bizarre? You have intrigued me, Sifu. And I am not easily intrigued. Why is it 'bizarre'?"

"I don't recall ever encountering such a mixture of character and personality types. Did you know Wayne McPeak and Hugo Garcia well?"

"I did not know them at all. Why do you ask?"

"Because they were killed today."

"My goodness. Two men who are apparently associated with Adam Chang are dead. How did they die?"

"I'm afraid that I killed them. They had announced their intention to kill my friends and me. We were not armed. They both were. It would not have been sufficient simply to try deter their attack."

"I see. Deadly force was necessary. I know a little Gung Fu. Certain pressure points, Dim Mak. Death blows. Yes, and you have studied Gung Fu?"

"Karate Dao."

"How extraordinary. Well, Sifu, I certainly hope you do not burden yourself with guilt. I'm sure it was karma. We are all subject to the laws of karma."

"Indeed." He ordered himself to stop looking at her body. "Have you heard anything about drug trafficking down on that Montoya land?"

Before Sonya Lee could answer, Wang Tai Tai wheeled in a tea cart. She poured two cups of tea. She did not ask Sensei if he wanted to drink a cup. She merely said, "This is special tea from Shao Guan in Guang Dong Province. It is served to guests at Nan Hua Temple. Do you know Nan Hua Temple?"

"Yes," he said, accepting the cup and saucer she handed him. "It's the Vatican of Zen Buddhism. I belong to a lineage of a nearby monastery, Yun Men."

"Indeed! That is marvelous. But tell me more about the drug trafficking," Sonya Lee said as the housekeeper handed her a cup and saucer and wheeled the cart out of the room.

"I'm looking for answers. I haven't found any yet."

"You strike me as the kind of man who will find what he looks for."

"I hope I am."

"The music is beautiful, isn't it?"

They listened to the ancient melodies as they sipped their tea. Sensei felt confused and did not know what to ask about drug trafficking. He finished his tea but had no place to set down the cup and saucer that rattled as his hand trembled with the unfamiliarity of just about everything that confronted him. There was a small footstool under the chaise longue. He pulled it closer to him with his foot. He bent forward trying to place the cup and saucer on the footstool; but the tea had drugged him, and he toppled from the chair onto the floor.

SUNDAY, JUNE 12, 2011

Martin was awakened early when Deputy Peterson called from his home near Las Flores. "You wanted to know where Adam Chang was taken. I found out. Memorial Hospital in Tucson."

Martin thanked him. "What's going on at the crime site?"

"I think they're crawlin' all over it. Takin' tests. Di'ja ever get that scorpion tie?"

"Yes, I did. Buy I'd like to get a few more... for friends."

"You can get them in Las Flores, at the General Store."

Martin called his grandfather. "I need to tell you about a few things that just happened to me." He sat on his bed and related the adventure at the Montoya land. "I wanted you to hear it from me."

Beryl awakened wondering where Sensei was. She had a hunch that her references to Ms. Sonya Lee's beauty had so intrigued Sensei that he went to her apartment to see for himself whether she was, in fact, that lovely. It also helped that she remembered that he had asked her for Ms. Lee's address. She called Sonya Lee's phone but no one answered.

"My guess," said Beryl, "is that the three of them are together."

"Would he go off like that," Martin asked, "without consulting you?"

"We have much more than a professional relationship. He's my Zen priest and my karate teacher. We have no secrets, and over the years we've developed a silent 'thought rapport.'"

"Do you want to go out for breakfast?" Martin asked. "I talked to my grandfather and told him about the incident in Las Flores. He told me that he's checking out a fire that occurred in Mesquite, Nevada… at a property that was owned by the Tres Amigos Old Spirits partnership."

"A fire? What? Like burning the joint down for insurance purposes?"

"He will let me know the details. He says it's complicated. So, do you want to go out to eat? We can talk about it."

"No," she answered. "I'm too worried to eat. You go if you want to eat. I'll call George and tell him all that's happened."

"I can't go into a restaurant like this. My shirt is filthy. So are my jeans."

"I probably don't have anything clean, either. Give me one of your shirts and a pair of your jeans. I'll take my shower now and wash your stuff and mine before I call George. Then we can go out to eat."

He wanted to ask how she expected to wear clothing that she had just washed, but he thought that it would turn out to be a stupid question. He handed her his jeans and shirt. "I do have clean underwear," he said.

"You're wearing underwear under your jeans? That is so 'yesterday.'"

In the morning, Sensei did not know where he was. He knew that he was confined in a very small dark room - a closet perhaps - and that his hands and feet were bound. A line of light against the floor indicated that a lamp or the sun was shining outside the little room. He roused himself and tried to reconstruct the last events he could remember. For the next half hour he passed in and out of consciousness, until he was at last able to stay awake and to think coherently. He began to notice a strange "ocean" scent in the air and he wondered if the odor had emanated from garments and boots that were on the floor near him.

Sensei could hear Chinese being spoken outside the room. Remembering the scent of incense in Sonya Lee's apartment, he put his nose down to the narrow space under the door and sniffed the air. He was definitely not in her apartment. The place had the unmistakable smell of dead fish. The door opened and two men who had not bothered to mask their faces - an inauspicious sign, Sensei knew - grabbed him and jabbed a needle into his thigh. The last thing he remembered thinking was that he could not decide if they were oriental or American Indian. If they were oriental, he decided, they were from the south. Their eyes were too wide to be northern.

Beryl brought the washed shirts and jeans to the patio and hung them on coat hangers. A palo verde tree's branches extended over the wall above the patio. She hooked the hangers onto the branches and returned to the bathroom to blow dry her hair into a passable style.

She had hoped that during the time of the shower and laundering, Sensei would call. He didn't. She called George. "Tell me everything that's happened," he said.

For nearly an hour they discussed the case. George tried to reassure her. "If there's one thing Sensei knows how to do, it's take care of himself. You're a professional. You can't worry about someone pointlessly. The best thing to do to help Sensei is to solve the goddamned case. The sooner, the better. You know the drill. Begin and continue."

It didn't help. "I'm sitting here with Martin and the two of us feel like hell. I don't know what to do next."

"Adam's partners need to be looked at. You already got the two guys who set up Adam Chang. But who put them up to it? Go interview the partners. It will take your mind off Sensei's problems."

Beryl kept George on the phone as she asked Martin if he wanted to drive up to Phoenix and call on Ivan Onegin."

"Why not?" he replied. "I'll go take my shower now. On the way we can visit Adam in Memorial Hospital and maybe check out Sonya Lee's place."

George heard the suggestion. "Good idea. Stop worrying. Keep busy with constructive stuff. Let me know the progress."

They drove north to Tucson. Their first stop was the Lorean Apartments. Sonya Lee's apartment gave no indication that anyone was home. They walked into the interior courtyard and looked up at her window. It was closed.

"I'm guessing that Sensei's with her," Beryl sighed. "And since Wang Tai Tai is not home either, I'm getting more and more worried."

They went to Memorial Hospital and asked for Adam Chang's room. The receptionist smiled and asked them if they would be kind enough to wait a moment. Five minutes later she returned to say that she could not find out whether or not she was supposed to give them any information.

Beryl baited her. "Don't tell me we just missed him!"

"Oh, no," she whispered, "he was taken out before breakfast."

"Oh. His parents said that they wanted to move him."

"The two gentlemen who pushed the wheelchair weren't his parents. He looked Chinese and they weren't Chinese. But they were nice and well dressed."

"Ah, government men."

"Probably. And they didn't say where they were going."

They got onto the interstate and headed for Phoenix, a two hour drive north.

Sensei did not know how long he had been unconscious. He did know that he had been moved and that his restraints had been changed from plastic to tightly tied cotton rope. He was now in a boat, in some kind of dark, covered box that was only a few feet square. His legs were bent. His head could touch his knees. From the unmistakable odor of fish, he knew that it must be a fishing boat of some kind. He could hear the engines and feel the easy bobbing of pitch and roll which led him to conclude that the boat was probably empty. He wondered how big the vessel was. He could only visualize the fleets of fishing boats he had seen in various ports. Maybe a five man crew, he thought, anywhere between thirty and forty feet in length. He felt his wrist ties and determined that they had been expertly knotted. A seaman, perhaps, had secured his wrists and ankles. But why had rope been substituted for the plastic zip ties? He could not imagine a reason for changing them. This bothered him. Why would anyone do that? Did someone think that cotton rope was biodegradable and that if his bones were discovered lying on the sea floor no one would be able to assume that he had been murdered? He was still groggy. Don't be ridiculous, he told himself. Biodegradable rope. Stupid. But if not that, what? He began to experience motion sickness and started to retch and to spit up bile. His gagging attracted the attention of someone outside. A tarp was lifted off the box and momentarily the light hurt his eyes. It was Wang Tai Tai.

"Good morning, Sifu," she said. "How you feeling today?"

"I'm sick... as you can see."

"Ah, well, we will be stopping soon to let you out. But first you tell us some things. You answer questions."

"What do you want to know?"

"Are you D.E.A. man?"

"No. I don't work for any government in any capacity."

"Then why you pretend to be Chinese Buddhist Priest and shave your head."

"I'm not pretending. I was ordained in Kaohsiung and reaffirmed in Shao Guan."

"If you are Chan Buddhist priest, you know Dharani to Guan Yin."

"Of course."

"Please recite."

"Na mu ka ra tan no to ry ya ya--"

"This is Japanese! This is not Chinese! You fake Buddhist priest."

Sensei retched again. "No, I am not. I teach karate. I follow Japanese style martial arts and the Japanese Zen Buddhist liturgy."

Someone called from the deck. Wang Tai Tai pulled the tarp down. In darkness again, Sensei suddenly heard Sonya Lee's voice. He did not understand what she was saying, but then he heard her footsteps get louder.

The tarp lifted and Sonya Lee looked down at him ferociously, "You bloody fool! You have just blown this operation! I hope I can get us out of this, you meddling nitwit!"

"Get me a knife!" he snarled. "And who the hell *are* you?"

"I'm with Hong Kong Customs. I don't see a knife around here." She saw a few woodcarving tools on a shelf. "A chisel?"

"Fine... get it!"

Sonya Lee tossed the chisel down into the box. "Keep your mouth shut and don't try to play the hero!" She slapped the tarp down on the box and again he was in darkness.

Sensei immediately wrapped the fingers of his right hand around the handle and began to rub the chisel's blade against the rope that secured his left wrist. The engine noise abated and the ship stopped moving. Sensei's stomach felt like a bobbing cork. "We're in neutral," Sensei thought. "We've stopped."

A man's authoritative voice commanded, "Release the drogue!" Another male voice answered, "Aye!" and Sensei began to feel a slight vibration and the tiny staccato beat of metal on metal as the thin chain of a canvas funnel slid into the water. "We're at sea," he told himself, "and in water too deep for an anchor to reach bottom."

Nearby, Wang Tai Tai's voice shouted, "I stay at wheel. You go aft! Keep watch. I leave running lights on! We wait." Sensei heard a man wearing heavy boots step down a couple of steps and then walk by, brushing the box he was in as he passed. The man opened a door and closed it. "I'm in the cabin of a fishing boat," Sensei thought. He rubbed the chisel against the rope but could not prevent the blade from nicking his flesh. The chisel's handle became bloody and difficult to hold. Finally, he cut through the rope and brought his hands around to the front where he could free his feet and complete the removal of the rope from his wrists.

He knelt in the box and pushed up a corner of the tarp, just enough to be able to see into the cabin. Wang Tai Tai sat in a swiveling chair in front of the wheel. A woman's footsteps passed by the box, stopped, and tapped the corner of the tarp that Sensei had lifted. "She knows I'm looking out," he thought and, for a reason he did not understand, he giggled and pushed the tarp up again.

Wang Tai Tai pulled Sonya down onto her lap. "Mei Mei," she said repeatedly as she nibbled Sonya's ear. Sonya put both of her arms around the older woman's neck and kissed her hard on the mouth. She began to make passionate groaning sounds that quickly increased in intensity. "Mei Mei!" repeated the older woman as she unbuttoned Sonya's blouse and began to kiss her breasts. Sonya sighed passionately and looked directly at the uplifted corner of the tarp. "Ohhh," she said, closing her eyes.

"Damn!" Sensei whispered. "She's doing that for my benefit!" Again he inexplicably giggled. He had known many women in his life, but none had ever fascinated him before. He did not care to analyze the novel experience. "Damn!" he whispered as Sonya made passionate gestures and pawed the older woman, while occasionally looking at the corner of the tarp and winking.

Ivan Onegin's home, a sprawling ranch style house that sat in the middle of two acres of Scottsdale's outer-edge desert, possessed no driveway gate to bar their way. Beryl swung off the road and, guided by a long row of half-buried recently produced wagon wheels, proceeded directly to the "nouveau-rustic" entrance. An area off to the side suggested itself as the place to park. She pulled in.

A blonde young man in his mid-twenties answered the door. "May I help you?" he asked.

"Mr. Onegin?" she inquired.

"No. I'm Enrique Montoya. Mr. Onegin's guest."

Beryl was surprised. She had supposed that the tall dark haired man in Chang's photograph was Montoya and the Russian named man was the blonde. "I'm Beryl Tilson. We've spoken on the phone." She surreptitiously switched on her digital voice recorder.

"Of course. We finally meet! *Miss* Tilson, isn't it?" He moved aside and indicated that she should enter. "And you are?" he stared at Martin.

"Adam Chang's attorney. Martin Mazzavini."

"I'm surprised to see you here."

"I'm sure you are," Martin said flatly.

Enrique Montoya nodded, indicating that Martin should enter, too. "Please, join us on the patio." As they walked toward the rear of the building, he turned his attention to Martin. "Are you a local man?"

"No," said Martin casually as he strode forward in his cowboy boots, trying to create a *born in the saddle* look. "I'm from Chicago."

"I'm just in from Santa Fe," Enrique said. "We were talking on the patio; but just before you knocked Ivan went into his bedroom to take a call from his parents. I don't know where the servants are. I'll make you a drink, myself. What'll you have?"

"Iced tea, if you have it," Beryl replied.

"Make that two," Martin added.

"Ah. No alcohol. You're working and driving."

Beryl stood in the kitchen doorway while Enrique removed a pitcher of iced tea from the refrigerator and filled two glasses. "I'll let you add the sugar or sweetener," he said, handing one to her. "There are several kinds out there on the patio... and spoons." He carried Martin's glass out to him.

As they sat down, Ivan Onegin's tall frame appeared in the doorway. "Sorry to be occupied when you knocked," he said, extending his hand. "I called Enrique yesterday and invited him to come since the case had become so newsworthy."

Beryl smiled. "This is Mr. Martin Mazzavini of Chicago. He's Adam Chang's attorney. Martin, this is Ivan Onegin, Adam's business partner." Martin stood up.

"Former business partner," Onegin corrected as he shook hands. "What can we do for you?"

"You might offer some kind of explanation as to why you haven't been attending to your... former... partner who's been suffering greatly of late," Beryl said in a matter-of-fact tone.

"First of all," Onegin answered, "the partnership has been dissolved. By agreement, it had a one-year term and without a unanimous vote to renew that term, it expired. For obvious reasons it could not be renewed." He stirred his tea and sat down. "How is Adam? We saw in the news that he's been transferred into a prison hospital of some kind. We didn't know which hospital. Do you know which hospital?"

"I'm intrigued," Beryl said. "When he was your partner you didn't care to visit him. But now that he's no longer a business associate, you'd... what? ... like to send him a get well card?"

Montoya entered the exchange. "We were in business with Adam Chang not Aaron Chin. If Adam didn't get many visitors he has only his pseudonym to blame. We did try to visit Adam. I already explained that to you. Speaking for myself, the nature of the charges and the place of his arrest could hardly induce me to drape myself and my family name all over him and his problems."

Onegin seconded the sentiment. "My father's a prominent businessman here in Arizona. We have to be particularly careful about associating with persons accused of drug trafficking."

"Adam is not charged with drug trafficking," Beryl said casually. "Are you afraid of associating yourself with persons *not* charged with drug trafficking? I don't see your point."

Martin placed his glass on the table. "Tell us more about the dissolution of your partnership. When was it officially dissolved? Do you have documentation to that effect?"

Montoya became conciliatory. "Let's not be so stiff and formal. There's no need for animosity. At the outset of our venture, we had every reason to be encouraged. We were all set to produce a high quality mezcal. Adam contributed his patented formula and method for producing a nearly congener-free beverage. Congeners are the distillation by-products - the fusel oils - that cause hangovers. Usually when you try to filter these out, you lose flavor; but in Adam's formula, there was an enhancement of flavor. We had high hopes for our venture. Booze that doesn't give you headache hangovers is a great thing. Still we decided that it was in all our interests to put a life span on the agreement. None of us had ever run a business before. Yes, if it had been another kind of business we certainly would have had family and friends to turn to for advice. But none of us knew anyone who was remotely familiar with producing alcoholic beverages.

"There's more to producing a bottle of mezcal than you might imagine. We recognized our inexperience. We each contributed something of value to the enterprise and with good reason were confident we could produce that bottle of mezcal. But could we market it? Distribute it? Get it through all of that incredible amount of regulatory paperwork that it required? Manage a successful mezcal business? We just didn't know. So we drew up a partnership agreement that gave us the latitude to try and, if the future looked promising, to continue, and if it didn't, to end it and walk away. Adam knew that unless we renewed the agreement, it would end, and ownership of the pledged assets, subject to the satisfaction of liens and other financial commitments, would return to the status quo ante."

Martin's pulse rate quickened. "I'd like to see those documents. If you don't have them, I'd like the name of the attorney who handled the partnership's creation and dissolution."

"I have them here," Onegin said, without moving. "Adam should have his set of copies, too. Can't he supply you with them?"

"I'm afraid not. All of his files and possessions are now in federal custody. I suppose I could petition the U.S. Marshal…" He had no idea whether the U.S. Marshal would be the correct bee's cell in the government's massive honeycomb to poke at, but it sounded authoritative.

Montoya looked at Onegin and jerked his head as if to say, "Do it!" Onegin stood up. "I'll make you copies of the agreement."

"And also a copy of the dissolution's 'satisfaction of liens and commitments.' I'm particularly interested in seeing that."

Onegin balked. He turned and stood in the doorway, looking contemptuously at Martin. "Am I your secretary?"

"Relax, Ivan," Martin said. "I don't fuck my secretary."

"Make him the goddamned copies!" Montoya snapped.

"All right," Beryl said. "Enough of this polite bickering. Let's wait for Mr. Onegin to return with the copies and then we can talk like normal folks who have a common interest. First, may I use your lady's room?"

"Follow me," Onegin said.

For five minutes Martin and Montoya sat in complete silence, listening to doors open and close, a copy machine run, a toilet flush, and footsteps returning the two missing "folks with a common interest" to the patio.

"I'll vouch for the complete accounting of the files. You have all the documents," Onegin said, handing them to Martin.

"Thank you," Martin said, pushing them into Beryl's tote bag.

Beryl cleared her throat and spoke pleasantly. "What's the history behind all this terrible trouble? The cause of the effect? Please. Let's start with March of last year or before that if it is relevant. And please, we're both tired, and as you can see, Mr. Mazzavini has been injured in the course of this investigation. Adam Chang and his family had their year in hell. He will find redress in both civil and criminal court. You two gentlemen may not be comfortable discussing the matter with us now, but if you don't you'll force us to consult the press and your respective families." Then she looked at Onegin and let her voice become comically stern, "While going to the bathroom I saw your family photographs in which your father is shown. I must now assert in the interests of full disclosure that I recognize him as 'Reese, your man from Sonoma House Real Estate' from whom my mother-in-law purchased a house in Chandler fifteen years ago." She pointed at Martin and began to sing an advertising jingle, "'If your house is getting crowded, and you'd like a little peace, come on down to our house, and meet a man named Reese.'"

Onegin yelled, "Foul! Foul! God, my youth was destroyed by that stupid song!"

Beryl tried to remember the rest of the song. "La la privacy and peace, la la pleasure you'll increase." She laughed along with Onegin. Then she looked at Montoya and said, "This man here (she pointed at Martin) is wearing seventeen hundred dollar python boots. Ya' wanna argue with him?"

Onegin went behind the bar and brought out a bottle of wine. "I've got one good bottle of Cabernet Sauvignon left. If you promise never to sing that song again you can have a glass." He poured four glasses. "Now that we're all here and Martin's got his copies, what do you want to know?"

"When did you form the partnership?"

"In March 2010. Before we could harvest the first crop of agave, Adam was arrested. We didn't know where he was; and although we had the plant ready to receive the first truckload of raw material, Adam had to be there to supervise the preparation. I didn't even know if we were supposed to wash the agave, or, if so, with what we were supposed to wash it. That was his job - at least to begin with. Without him, we couldn't go on."

Martin sipped the wine. "Good stuff. Did you have partnership insurance on him?"

"Yes," Montoya answered, "we did. It was routine insurance. Nothing out of the ordinary."

"How much did you collect?" Martin swirled the wine in his glass. After a pause, Montoya said, "Two million each."

"When did you file the claim?"

"The partnership agreement stipulated that if a partner failed to perform his operational duties for a period of one hundred twenty continuous days, the other partners could collect. In the fine print it lists 'incarceration' as well as 'death' or any medical reasons. The only exception was being drafted into the armed forces or by any other act of Congress or something. I can assure you we were entitled to file that claim."

"When did you file the claim?"

"Last fall."

"That entitled you to collect the partnership insurance, but not to terminate the partnership. When did you do that?" Martin asked.

"When the year was up... in March. We are no longer involved with Adam in any business arrangement."

"And the disposition of his assets... the patent on his process that he contributed as his part of the initial investment?"

"Creditors were owed money. We hired workers. There were insurance costs on the building. There was an investment in office fixtures and equipment. There were numerous filing fees and costs incurred in filing documents. Nobody works for nothing. We had to turn on telephone service, water, gas, electricity. You didn't expect me to pay for all that just because I owned the building."

"No more than I would expect a disproportionate share of it to be levied against my client," Martin said. "I'll review the documents."

Montoya sighed and sipped his wine. "It's important to realize that we didn't *act*. We *reacted*. We fulfilled our commitments and then things happened and we responded to the changes. It was a calamity, the destruction of a dream." He sipped his wine again. "Perhaps we made a few mistakes. But we were victims. We deserve a little understanding and not all this hostility."

"May we personalize those mistakes?" Beryl asked. "What, Mr. Montoya, were your mistakes?"

"Oh, Jesus! I don't see what purpose this will serve!"

"There is considerably more going on here and nobody wants to discuss it. There was a fire in that plant in Mesquite, Nevada. Who bore the costs of that fire? Tell us about the fire? What did the fire department's report say? Gentlemen, do we look like we're getting ready to pack up and run?" Beryl lifted her glass and looked at him. "Either we get the story from you, or..."

Montoya stood up. "This is painful," he said. "All right. I won't try to sugar coat it." He hesitated, "Is this going to be made public?"

"Maybe," suggested Martin, "you should talk to your own attorneys if you feel that your interests are going to be compromised. If you did anything criminal, you definitely should have counsel."

"Ivan and I are so sorry that we ever got mixed up in this."

Beryl stared at him incredulously. "Mixed up with Adam Chang?"

"This whole mezcal business."

"That *means* Adam Chang! And *you're* sorry? We're prepared to hear your side of the story. If you don't want to give it, fine. We'll get it from the newspapers and instead of wine we can serve—"

"Subpoenas?" Montoya asked. "Is that what you were going to say? Nobody needs to summon us. This whole story is stupid and no doubt it's stupid because we let it get out of control. I am most to blame. Not Adam or Ivan. Me. All right. I'll tell you the whole story. It's deeply personal, but I see that you don't care about sensitive things like that.

"When we went to Las Flores last year looking for Adam, we talked to law enforcement personnel and learned just how much trouble he was in. The last thing either of us needed was a scandal. I don't expect you to understand the kind of pressure we were under. Neither Ivan's family nor mine wanted us to have anything to do with making an alcoholic beverage. Ivan's a Mormon and my great-grandfather drank away a considerable fortune.

"But both of our families have had money for generations. Adam was a scholarship student. Friends warned us about being tied to someone outside our financial stratum. When people try to keep up with a person financially, they'll bend a lot of rules. In Las Flores, we learned just how far those rules had been bent. We believed what we heard. So we were stuck with our plans to make money in the mezcal trade. Once cocaine entered the mix, it became a nightmare for us. You would have to understand family pressure. Relatives can really lay on the abuse.

"So, all right. Maybe we were too quick to accept defeat. Maybe it was convenient to be gullible. Whatever! We were relieved to put an end to the whole mezcal business." He sat back in his chair.

"And?" Beryl asked. "What about the fire?"

"Christ! All right. I had thought that I had clear title to the land. I had the legal description, the metes and bounds, and I knew the recording numbers of the deed, and so on, so I never actually went and got the deed out of the vault. My grandfather had led me to believe that I was the sole owner. In fact, I owned the land jointly with my kid sister, Valentina. I have a sister who's not exactly unintelligent and bi-polar but, well, lonely and emotionally erratic and sometimes a little slow. She goes to a special private school for girls. A Catholic school. I owned only half of the land committed to our Tres Amigos partnership. When I finally realized my mistake, it no longer mattered since Adam was in jail. And frankly, the land was worth much more than my share of the asset pool would have been.

"Ivan and I went about our business and tried to get past the whole nightmarish episode, and then, last fall, Ivan's father, Reese of the Sonora House jingle fame, told me he had a prospective buyer, a gentleman who wanted to buy the land to use as a residence, a hacienda. He wanted to raise a few horses and cattle. A gentleman rancher. We weren't interested in selling, but he persisted and said that the client was going to be in Santa Fe in another week and wanted to discuss the purchase. Out of consideration for Ivan's dad, my father told me to invite the man to the house for dinner.

"You don't want to hear all this."

"Yes, we do. It's interesting," Beryl said, taking out her little blue tablet.

"He turned out to be a young guy, a decent fellow named Harley... Harley Saint John only it is pronounced Sinjin. The British way, although he had no British accent. But you don't want to hear about him."

Beryl interrupted him. "Yes, we do. Tell us about Harley. He sounds fascinating."

Montoya continued. "He was well spoken and educated. He seemed to get a kick out of my kid sister, Valentina. We have a garden and she took him around and told him the names of all the flowers and the little mythic stories that went with them. Silly stuff. But he seemed to eat it up. My father said it wouldn't hurt to get the land appraised."

Ivan Onegin groaned. "I need another drink." He got up and went to the bar. "This is where I get into the act," he said. "At the time of this biosphere bull, I was losing a lot of money trying to maintain an idle distillery. You can't have rats running around a place that processes food of any kind. So I was being drained. A potential buyer for the distillery turned up. He was interested in the wine industry that was taking off in Nye County, Nevada. My father, acting as my agent, met this gentleman from Buenos Aires. He took him to Nevada where he sees all this great equipment sitting there and he's sold. *But* he wants to buy the agave land as well as the distillery. This is a problem because Harley St. John is becoming a regular house guest in Santa Fe. He's romancing Enrique's sister who is the 'baby doll' of the family."

"And then," Enrique Montoya got up and walked to the edge of the patio. When he spoke he seemed to be speaking over his shoulder, not wanting anyone to see his face. Beryl noted his strange body language. "And then," he repeated, "there was talk of marriage between Harley and my sister. She was crazy about him, so I told her that I'd give her my half of the land as her eighteenth birthday present - which would have to be before any wedding ceremony so that it wouldn't be community property. We didn't want to make this gift public because it would seem as if we were 'inducing' Harley to marry my sister. The land was appraised at four million. Harley didn't have enough money to buy it, and to tell the truth, we really had no intention of selling it to him. It wasn't that we thought that there was a chance the Tres Amigos could harvest the agave and produce mezcal. No. That dream had ended. We didn't want Harley to have it because my father didn't want Valentina living so far away in the Sonora desert. He owned a beautiful ranch near Taos that he wanted to give them as a wedding present. And again, he didn't mention this to anyone but me because it would look like he was buying my sister a husband.

"Ravenel is set to buy both properties--"

"--Who is Ravenel?" Beryl asked.

"Gustavo Ravenel, the buyer for the distillery. My father and Ivan's father think they've struck gold. My sister is so in love with a decent man who wants to marry her. You can't imagine how much this means to us... this was a miracle to my parents. We get rid of that cursed piece of land in Las Flores and Ivan gets rid of the distillery and the new box truck. Escrow accounts are opened in Nye County and in Pima County. Upon meeting certain conditions, the deal will go forward.

"We didn't expect Harley to object - not when we told him about the Taos property. But he goes berserk. He wants that land and he insists that it's been promised to him. It was supposed to be the dream ranch for him and Valentina. This upsets my father because there was no deal in place. They argue and Harley leaves in a fit of anger. And suddenly there's a fire at the distillery. It's arson and two different security cameras and his rented car's GPS place Harley at the scene. The sheriff gets on it fast and Harley's arrested in a motel with the smell of gasoline still on him. Ravenel looks at the burned out building and says, 'Adios,' and that's still not so bad because Ivan had insured the building." He stopped talking and began to walk to the path that led down into the grass beyond the patio.

"Are you then back to Square One?" Beryl asked.

"No," Ivan said. "Enrique doesn't want to talk about it. I'm back to Square One, but Enrique's troubles are just beginning. When Harley was sitting in jail in Nye County, Nevada, Valentina convinces a nun and another schoolmate to go with her to Nye County to visit him. He's held on one million dollars bail and is waiting for someone to come up from Arizona to bail him out. Valentina has told him that she'll get the Las Flores land for a wedding present. He thinks it is a win-win situation. It's easy to get married in Nevada. He tells her to wait for him in a motel. She and the nun and the classmate are missed at school. There's a scandal. He gets bailed out of jail and goes to the motel and the same sheriff who arrested him for arson arrests him for statutory rape and the Mann Act or something, and contributing to the delinquency of a minor, and it goes on and on. Enrique's father and the father of the other girl as well as the Mother Superior of the School have to go to Nye County and get the women. There is no bail for Harley, now. And when Ricky's father tells Harley that he'd sooner burn in hell than have his daughter marry him, Harley turns on Valentina and humiliates her in front of everyone. Cruel doesn't describe what he said. Her heart is broken. She's so humiliated that she literally becomes catatonic. She's still in the hospital. The nun was expelled or disciplined in some way. And it goes on and on and on. And *then* it goes back to Square One."

Beryl closed her tablet and put it into her purse. "I have a question. Why did Harley want the land in the first place? Obviously, he was not a gentleman rancher."

"I don't know. After the murders and the cocaine business I figured maybe drugs had something to do with it. The land goes right up to the Mexican border. Maybe he wanted it as a private drug corridor. I just don't know. The Montoyas never understood it, either."

"One more thing," Ivan said. "I had mortgaged the distillery. I was obliged to let the insurance company restore it. I've since paid off the mortgage. So I have a nice vacant distillery, in case you know anyone who's interested."

"What can I say?" Beryl asked. "Things have a way of getting complicated."

Martin and Beryl prepared to leave. Martin said, "You guys should definitely get yourself legal counsel. The Montoya land may very well figure in a drug smuggling operation. This Harley person may be involved in the murder and now he has another connection to you. There will be a conference in Tucson on Friday. You should be present. Either the D.A.'s office or I will call you with the time and place details. I'm advising you to attend. It goes better when it's voluntary. Other than that you'll be subpoenaed. I'm truly sorry to hear about Montoya's kid sister. I hope she recovers."

When they pulled out of Onegin's driveway, Martin stared into Beryl's tote bag until she got the message that she was to turn the recorder off. She reached into the bag and clicked off the device. Martin smiled. "Those arrogant bastards. If they had anything to do with setting Adam up so that they could collect on the partnership agreement, I'm gonna see them fry. Ok. Let's ask George to find out what he can about Gustavo Ravenel. I'll look through these partnership documents while you drive. But as soon as you see a place that faxes stuff, pull in. I've got to send these to my grandfather."

"Whether or not they defrauded the insurance company, they still tried to sell off the partnership's assets while the agreement was in effect. Do I have that right?"

As Martin skimmed through the documents, she called George and left a message. "Could you run down Gustavo Ravenel of Buenos Aires?" She spelled the last name. "He's probably in the drug trade."

Martin looked up. "As I read it, they couldn't touch those assets until the one year termination. They may have tried to force the sale of Adam's patent in order to pay off the expenses they incurred. In that case, you can be sure they will be participating in the new ownership. Wow... they really screwed this kid. Tres Amigos. When are people gonna learn that 'three's a crowd.' He never had a chance one way or the other. Montoya lied to us throughout. And so did Onegin."

"It's funny. I never knew Reese's last name. I always thought it was Reese." She began to sing, "'If your house is getting crowded and you'd like a little peace--'"

"Aaargh! I surrender. No more. No more. I'll sic that Scarpio on ya.'"

A ship's horn sounded. Sensei thought it must be close by. He waited, listening intently to every sound he could hear. He heard and felt a smaller boat being lowered. It banged and scraped against the hull. He watched as Sonya Lee tried to pull away from Wang Tai Tai. The older woman whined and begged her to stay longer. Sonya Lee looked in Sensei's direction, secretly puckered her lips into a kiss, and demurely buttoned her blouse.

"You are such a devil!" he whispered under his breath. It did not surprise him that he felt no fear or even concern about his predicament. His legs were cramping, but aside from that and a few small cuts on his hands, the only subject that occupied his thoughts was the woman who had been kissing another woman while she winked at him. "Damn!" he continued to repeat. Sonya went forward into the partitioned bridge. He could hear her operating a communication device of some sort. She spoke in Chinese.

Wang Tai Tai went aft, brushing Sensei's box as she passed it. He lifted the tarp higher and looked around the cabin. On a shelf he saw a pair of red high-heeled shoes. Sonya was wearing deck shoes, but the heels, he decided, were definitely hers.

He could hear the older woman order someone to open a hatch. He heard a heavy metal object thud against the wooden deck. She ordered a man to go down into the hold and hand up the cargo. Another man received what sounded like boxes that he stacked on the deck. Fifteen minutes passed. The hatch was put back and secured.

The man whose boots he had first heard walked past him to the bridge. Sensei peeked and saw him pull open a drawer and remove something which he put in his pocket. The man returned and exited the cabin. Sensei could hear the two men descend the rope ladder and board the small boat that continued to bang against the hull. Its motor started, lines were tossed, and the boat sped away. By Sensei's reckoning, Sonya and Wang Tai Tai were on the fishing boat, alone, with him. He expected the tarp to be lifted, but Sonya walked past him without acknowledging his presence in the box. The two women were alone on the working deck.

He heard the engine of another, larger boat approach. The engine's sound suddenly lessened as it dropped into neutral and idled. Someone on the approaching vessel shouted, "Ahoy! Mickeyfin!" Sonya shouted, "Ahoy!" A line was tossed to Wang Tai Tai. Sensei could hear and feel the boat thump against the hull. Sonya called, "Olá!" One of the men returned the greeting as he climbed the rope ladder. Feet scuffled on deck.

Another man called, "Está listo?"

Sonya replied, "Sí. Hay mucha carga."

The man answered. "Qué tipo?" he asked, "y cuánto?"

"Doscientos kilos hashish. Cuatrocientos kilos coca. Todo lo que usted ordenó está aquí."

"*Bueno,*" the man said. "*Y dónde está el Capitán?*"

"*Está allí con ellos, hablando de dinero.*"

The man looked around the cabin. "*Dónde está la monja?*"

"*No hay monja. Hay un monje. Lo siento mucho. Él es mío. Lo siento por ese error.*"

"*Mi desgracia.*" He evidently grabbed Sonya in a playful way and said something about going "*conmigo.*" Sonya spoke Spanish to him. Suggestive Spanish, Sensei thought, judging from the throaty laugh that followed her words.

The cargo was quickly transferred to the smaller vessel. A line was tossed, the engine was dropped into gear, and the boat sped away. There was silence for another half hour and then Sensei heard the first motorboat approach. There were more bumper scrapings and the knocking together of two vessels and shouts as a hoisting apparatus was secured. Sonya passed through the cabin, and at the bridge she activated another engine that hoisted the small craft onto the deck. The captain and the man with heavy boots were aboard. The captain walked through the cabin and put a satchel into a cabinet close to where Sonya was standing.

Sensei tried to get himself into a variety of postures so that he could stretch his legs. His muscles were cramping badly. He had learned from Sonya's conversation with the man who spoke Spanish that he had somehow been saved from destruction by her "error" in mislabeling his sex. She had promised the men a female they could plunder but, unfortunately, the 'nun' had turned out to be a 'monk' - a curious coincidence, he thought - which she intended to keep for herself. "Damn!" he said, amused.

The horn of a very large vessel sounded in the distance, indicating its approach and intention to stop. It was probably a merchant ship of some kind, he thought. A tanker would not have stopped.

As near as he could determine, only Wang Tai Tai, Sonya, the captain, and the man with heavy boots, minus the cargo and plus the satchel, were now on the "Mickeyfin," assuming he had heard the fishing boat's name correctly called. He expected that the transaction had been concluded and that they would move. But nothing happened. He had been ordered to make no disturbance, and so he waited. "This," Sonya had said, "was her operation."

Wang Tai Tai entered the cabin and went directly to the wheel. "Did they give you all the money?" she asked the Captain.

"Yes. What di'ja think? That I let them give me an I.O.U.? Shut up and get back inside." He tried to communicate with someone on the ship's radio.

"I want to see the money," she replied.

"I want to weigh a hundred eighty pounds and be twenty-five."

"Where is the money?" Wang Tai Tai demanded.

"It's in the goddamned satchel stowed right in front of me." He kicked the door of a built-in cabinet. "Now shut up and get your ass off the bridge."

Sensei could not determine all of the words they spoke, but he did understand their tone, and this surprised him. He had assumed that Wang Tai Tai was a boss of some kind; but the captain, who was obviously in the same organization as she, did not show her the respect he would have shown a superior. He surmised that neither of them headed the operation.

"Why you don't bring up drogue?" she demanded.

"Because I'm not ready to leave just yet. I'll hoist the drogue when I'm ready!" He spoke again to someone on the radio. Sensei could not understand the language he spoke.

"Why we wait?" Wang Tai Tai shrieked. "Why you don't bring up drogue?" she shouted in the captain's ear.

The captain had been trying to hear something on an earphone. He suddenly raised his arm and flung Wang Tai Tai down the two steps that led into the galley. She lay on the floor, her back against the box Sensei occupied. The captain concluded his call and then followed her down into the cabin and kicked her. "Shut up, you old bitch! And do as you're told!"

Sensei could clearly hear her whimper and call for Sonya. The captain had returned to the bridge and also called for Sonya.

Sonya entered the cabin and paused to say something in Chinese to the older woman before she continued forward. "What's the holdup?" she asked.

"A surprise," the captain said, pulling her to him.

Wang Tai Tai began to talk to herself. She continued to mutter as she pushed herself up and got to her feet. From the corner of the box Sensei could see the older woman place a backpack on the galley table. She unzipped it and removed a metal box which she opened. She removed a syringe and a vial. She drew a cc of clear liquid into the syringe.

The mate entered the cabin and called. "Any contact yet?" He did not continue to walk through. Instead, he opened the refrigerator and took out a can of beer. "Wanna beer?" he called, holding the door open as he drank.

"Yeah," the captain said, "bring two. They're ready. Be here in half an hour." The mate shut the refrigerator door and went forward with the two cans. The captain was on the radio again. He ended his call and said, "Make sure the motorboat is secure." The mate snickered and started down the two steps to the cabin as the captain began to fondle Sonya.

Just as the mate passed the table, Wang Tai Tai turned and plunged the needle into his trachea, fiercely pushing it back until he was nearly lifted off his feet. He swung his arms, trying to force her to pull the needle out, but she held it firm, and with only a gurgling sound, he slowly dropped to the floor. Sensei could hear her chuckle in a sinister guttural voice as she whispered something to the fallen man. She pulled the syringe out of his throat and turned to open the little box that contained the vial. She drew another cc of liquid into the syringe. The captain heard a noise and called, "Tony!" She answered, "He go aft. What you want?"

The captain pushed Sonya away. "Is anything goin' on down there?" he called. "I'm gonna get that old bitch and throw her overboard!" He shoved Sonya aside. Wang Tai Tai confronted him. She stood on the first of the two steps and held the syringe high, as though it were a knife.

"No!" Sonya shouted.

The older woman paid no attention. She took another step, advancing toward the captain who laughed at her. He kicked her in the chest and she fell back onto the galley floor, stumbling over the mate's body. The captain jumped down and seeing the mate, grabbed her arm as she tried to stab him with the needle. He twisted her arm and pulled it and then stepped on it, breaking it as he would break a stick of firewood. She screamed. The syringe slid across the floor.

The captain, his chest heaving, cursed her and picked her up. She screamed as he carried her through the cabin and out onto the deck where he smashed her head against a winch's housing and threw her silent body into the sea. Sonya stayed at the wheel and said nothing.

He was still breathing hard as he returned to the bridge. "You wanna join her?" he shouted at Sonya.

"And why would I want to do that?" she sweetly asked. "Calm yourself. It isn't good for you to get so excited."

He drained the can of beer and belched. "Get me another beer!"

"Sure," she said. Then instantaneously her index and middle finger pierced his eyes. He yelped and grabbed his face. She kicked him in the groin and as he doubled over, she delivered a fierce strike to the base of his skull. Sensei recognized the move as a *kyusho jitsu* or *Dim Mak* death strike. The captain collapsed onto the floor. Sonya stepped over him and pulled off the tarp. "Time to earn your keep, Karate Man. Yes, I know who you are, Yao Feng."

Sensei tried to stand up. "Give me a goddamned minute. Couldn't you find a smaller box?"

"Get that blood circulating! A boat is on its way and we've got to get these guys below!"

Sensei needed time to get his legs moving properly before he could climb out of the box. He held on to the top edge of the box and jumped in place. "Is the hatch still open?" he asked.

"No. It's hard to open."

Sensei vaulted out of the box and hurried to the deck. Sonya went to the bridge and called someone on the radio as Sensei opened a hatch and returned to the cabin. He picked up the mate's feet and dragged his body out to the deck. Sonya ended her call and ran back to help push the mate down into the hold. "Are you sure he's dead?" he asked.

"Yes. She would have jabbed that curare right up into his brain. I'm serious. I've seen her do it."

They returned for the much heavier captain. Each of them grabbed one of his legs and slowly they pulled him through the cabin. They could hear a motor boat approaching. They pulled harder and got him on the deck and into the hold just as the motor boat dropped into neutral and drifted towards them. Sensei closed the hatch as Sonya went to the side to greet the oncoming vessel. "Ahoy!" she shouted and waved. Sensei stood beside her and made ready to receive their line. The boat was a sleek 'cigarette' racing boat. Two men stood up. In the glow of the Mickeyfin's running lights, Sensei could detect at least two other men. The two standing men waved, but turned and talked, making no move to toss them a line.

Sensei stood beside her. He quickly asked, "And just why did you put me in that box?"

"I told Mrs. Wang that I had promised the captain I'd bring him a toy. She and the captain have a little game they play with nosy cops. But Vince, the captain, wasn't in the mood to play today. He had his own plans. He was supposed to return to port with the payment for those drugs; instead he made a deal with an old competitor to deliver the money to him... the guy driving that cigarette boat."

"Why did you bring me?"

"I told you. If you had any gratitude in you, you'd thank me for saving your hide."

"What was the game?"

Sonya waved at the men. "Any problem?" she asked. To Sensei she said, "She puts a long chain on a padlock and puts the padlock around your scrotum and then tosses you in the water and makes you swim along with the boat."

"Ah. And you hold the chain?"

"No. It's tied onto the rail. She makes the captain speed up and then slow down. They find it strangely amusing."

"And you would do that to me? *Moi?*"

The cigarette boat dropped into gear and moved forward, making a large arc in the water.

"What are they doing?" Sensei asked.

"Because they were on the starboard side they probably feared that if they had to put that expensive boat into reverse it would pull to port. They usually pull to port." Sensei gave her a sideways look. "And they would back into our luxury liner. Or else they just thought that tying up on the starboard side would bring them bad luck."

"There are at least four guys in that speedboat," he said. "It doesn't look like they intended to take anything more than a satchel of money off this ship. Did you call for help?"

"Of course. We were prepared for this double cross but not quite at this time. You nearly ruined the whole operation. I hope you're happy. If we get help in time and make it back to shore I'm going to kick your karate-man ass."

"Just so you do it in red spiked heels. I've developed an interest in red spike-heeled shoes."

She watched as the boat pulled along side the fishing vessel's left side. "Welcome aboard!" she called to the two men who were beginning to climb the rope ladder. "You just missed the captain. He and Tony were called over to the big ship. They'll be back in a few minutes. You're Gebhardt, aren't you? I heard Tony mention your name."

"I don't like this," Gebhardt replied. "Vince just talked to me. He didn't say anything about going to the big ship." He saw the motorboat tied up on the side of the deck. Sonya noticed it, too.

"They sent a boat for him and Tony. After he radioed you, he got their call. What could he do? What's the hurry?"

Sensei remembered the syringe and went into the cabin to pick it up. He put it behind a canister near the stove. He cleaned off the galley table.

"Who's this guy?" Gebhardt asked, indicating Sensei.

"Special delivery. He's some kind of opium expert they're delivering to the guys in Juarez. Don't ask me what they want with him. What you don't know, you can't tell. He speaks English. I tried Chinese on him. He doesn't speak it. Would you like a cold beer?"

Gebhardt was not convinced. He left the cabin and went to the side to talk to the men in the cigarette boat. Sensei saw the two men stand up. He looked meaningfully at Sonya. She stood in the doorway and watched one of the men, an oriental, struggle to climb the rope ladder.

Sensei knew that she was thinking exactly what he was thinking. Four against two. Four armed against two unarmed. Gebhardt took her arm. "Where's the money?"

The other two men could not be allowed on deck. The man on the ladder had reached the top and was preparing to climb over the rail. Sensei came up along side Sonya and suddenly kicked Gebhardt in the lower back, sending him sprawling against the man whose leg was half way over the rail. Sonya immediately turned to the other man who was reaching for his gun. She grabbed his arm and twisted it, flipping him over onto his belly. He screamed as his arm tore loose from its socket. Gebhardt had had the wind knocked out of him and as he whooped trying to regain his breath, Sensei grabbed his foot, pulled it up, and tossed him over the rail. Sonya picked up the screaming man's gun and gave it to Sensei. As the man got onto his knees and tried to lunge for Sonya, Sensei shot him and he crumpled onto the deck. "Cover me," Sonya said. "I'm gonna start the engine. We'll drag them."

"Hoist the drogue!" Sensei called. "Immediately an engine started and the drogue's chain began to wind. Then Sonya started the ship's powerful Caterpillar engine and it began to move forward, pulling the cigarette boat along side.

Sensei looked down to see the man in the cigarette boat try to free it, but it had been tethered too securely. He saw the two men thrash in the water. Sonya again was talking on the ship's radio.

For half an hour Sonya circled the area. Sensei was becoming seasick. So was the man in the attached boat. Finally the helicopter lights came into view and a Coast Guard boat's siren could be heard in the distance. She had also informed the Coast Guard that the cigarette boat that was tied to the fishing vessel had a mother ship. Off in the distance, more helicopter and Coast Guard vessels could be seen, lights flashing.

Overhead, someone in the helicopter spoke on a bullhorn. The man in the cigarette boat was ordered to stand with his hands behind his head. An armed officer was lowered on a cable directly into the boat. Another man descended and landed on the Mickeyfin's deck. "Any sick or wounded?" he asked.

Sensei groaned.

"Do you want to be airlifted ashore?"

Sensei looked up at the helicopter. "God, no."

"There were two smugglers back there someplace... in the water," Sonya said. "They are possibly alive. We'll wait for your ship." She indicated a vessel that was heading for them.

The prisoner in the cigarette boat was taken up into the helicopter. As the aircraft sped into the night she turned to Sensei and asked, "'Hoist the drogue?' You don't know port from starboard and you say, 'Hoist the drogue!'"

"As you will soon discover," he said, "I am a man of many strange and mysterious powers."

MONDAY, JUNE 13, 2011

At six o'clock in the morning, Sensei called. "I've been up all night," he said, "here in Los Angeles, at the consulate of the People's Republic of China, sitting on a hard bench in the hall. I think that many of the problems associated with the arrest of Adam Chang have been solved. I'll tell you all about it when I get back."

"Are you with Sonya Lee?" Beryl asked.

"Yes. It's a long story. She's an agent with Hong Kong Customs... their Drug Enforcement Bureau. That housekeeper who worked for her was one of the drug runners. She funneled cocaine and hashish that came across the border from Mexico into ships that were bound for Hong Kong. She's dead, by the way."

"Wang Tai Tai? Uh, oh. Did you kill her?"

"No. The captain of the Mickeyfin - which is the boat I've been on - killed her. And then Sonya killed the captain; and then his confederates, who didn't know he was dead, came aboard looking for him and the payoff drug money. The captain was double-crossing his own boss. The cigarette boat people were his new partners. I did get one of those guys, and then the Coast Guard picked up the rest. Do you need me back there today? I'd really like a little time off to rest."

"Give me the gist of your madcap adventure. George will want to know."

Sensei related as much of the experience as he could remember. "I'll explain in more detail later. Right now a very pretty lady is coming down the hall headed for me."

"Ok. This is important. Ask Sonya if she knows anything about a guy who's a big drug trafficker... a guy named Gustavo Ravenel from Buenos Aires. He's in jail there now. After this case went public the Argentine authorities got him on a fugitive warrant. He was in 'Argentine waters' they said. And there's a big conference scheduled for Friday involving Martin and his grandfather and the district attorney, etc., etc., in Tucson. Miss Lee may be needed, too, if she's in a position to shed light on whatever has been going on down here. I'm sure she must have a DEA contact. We found out who Harley is. Harley St. John, pronounced 'sinjin' a.k.a. Harley McPeak. Tell her we need all she's got on the Montoya land smuggling operation. Bring her and the documents to the meeting. Call me for details. Tell her to also fax the stuff ASAP to Martin Mazzavini's Chicago office. Meanwhile, get some rest and have fun, fun, fun."

Sensei laughed. "I'll do my best."

"At last now I can get some sleep," Beryl said. She disconnected the call and speed-dialed George. On his voice mail she left the message, "Sensei's ok. He's in California."

Sensei's call had awakened Martin. He came through the open adjoining door and flopped on Beryl's bed. "I hope it's the medication," he said, "but I know I should be doing something. I can't think straight."

"You should call Adam Chang's parents and ask them to come here. And you should pay all their expenses."

"I don't even know where the hell Adam is. How can I call them? Suppose they ask."

"Then call and find out."

"Ask my opponents where my client is? That, Miss Tilson, is not done."

"Call the jail in Las Flores and ask Deputy Peterson if he knows. He told you the last time. Besides, the area may still be crawling with your forensic people. He may be inclined to get onto your side."

He called the jail.

Peterson was friendly. "How are you feelin'?" he asked. "I heard you got some bad burns from the truck bed."

"Yeah, it's worse than sunburn, but the soreness ought to go away within the week, they tell me. Is there anything going on at the Montoya property?"

"Yes, plenty. Yesterday and today. There were University guys there, and lab guys, and three or four pickup trucks, cameras, equipment. I think they're doing temperature readings. That's what my wife said, anyway. How's the kid?"

"I wish I could tell you. They moved him out of Memorial. Do you know where they took him?"

"Wait a minute. Some federal agents were using this office as their headquarters last night. The cleanin' gal may have overheard something." Martin heard him ask a woman if she remembered hearing where Adam was supposed to be taken. Peterson then spoke to Martin, "She thinks the feds took him up to Phoenix for a few days. Part protection and part to see some specialist they liked up there."

"Where did they take him?"

Peterson repeated the question to the cleaning lady. She thought a moment and then answered, "I think it was to some private clinic or small hospital. I can't remember the name."

Peterson said to Martin, "If it's the place I think it is, it's at I-17 and Pinnacle. It's on the left side of the freeway as you're goin' north. Do you want me to find out when they'll be bringing him back?"

"Nah. But if anythin' interestin' happens at the crime scene, gimme a call. I'd appreciate it."

Beryl stared at him. "Already you're becoming one of the 'good old boys?'"

"Yeah. Bubba Mazzavini. Peterson says they took Adam up to Phoenix, to a private hospital at I-17 and Pinnacle." He made a note in his blue tablet. "lft sd as ur go nor." He looked up and pronounced, "Left side as you're going north."

Beryl sat up. "That's interesting. And here I thought we could vegetate today." She yawned. "The drugs are really dulling my brain."

Martin looked at his tablet and tried to understand his own cryptic notes. It was useless. "My brain has turned to mush. I can't read my own goddamned writing." He looked at Beryl, wanting to ask her to help him decipher the abbreviations. She was asleep. He went into her shower and turned on the cold water. Then he returned to the bed and picked her up and carried her to the shower. "You need to wake up," he said. "You're driving."

"Again?"

"Yep!" he said. "We're moseyin' up to Phoenix."

Sonya Lee had wanted to howl for joy when she signed her last report and handed it to the consul. "I want to get into a tub and soak for a couple of hours," she said to one of the two bachelor agents who were attached to the consulate.

"I will be happy to wash your back," one said quietly. The consul heard the remark and scowled. He nodded, dismissing the two agents.

"I don't require any help, but thank you," Sonya whispered as the agent left.

"So who is the civilian, the Buddhist priest out there in the lobby?" the consul asked.

"It's all in my report, my dear. Read it." Sonya clearly was on friendly terms with the consul.

The consul returned his pen to its holder. "I'm tempted to call my Sifu back in Guang Zhou. There is supposed to be an American monk from a good Chinese family who studied Karate. A master of some sort. Pelsey, they call him. Pelsey Wang. But he teaches on the East Coast."

"He's the one. It's Percy. His Dharma name is Shi Yao Feng. Yun Men Temple. I promised I'd kick his ass for interfering with a government investigation."

"If he's the guy I'm thinking about, you're in for a workout."

Sonya Lee laughed and went out into the lobby to join Sensei.

Sonya had said, "I'm taking you home," and Sensei assumed that this meant a long drive back to Tucson. He followed her to an official black car expecting to be driven all the way to the Lorean Apartments. He was looking forward to the comforts of the apartment that now, in the absence of Wang Tai Tai, could be enjoyed.

Instead, Sonya Lee turned north and got onto the Pacific Coast Highway. "I have a beach house in Malibu," she said, in answer to Sensei's quizzical look. "We'll be there shortly. Call your people and find out when we have to be back."

"There will be some kind of conference on Friday. Beryl will call me as soon as she learns precisely when and where it will be. She humbly asks for any copies of any relevant documents that you may have and any information you may have about a few people."

"Tell me later," Sonya said. "Turn your phone off."

Sensei turned off his phone.

The Malibu house was small but furnished in a Danish modern style that Sensei appreciated. "Are you still going to kick my ass?" he asked.

"Do you like your ass kicked?" she answered.

"Only if you leave your red spike heels on," he answered. "I saw that you brought them with you."

Sonya laughed and kicked off her deck shoes, aiming perfectly for an open closet door. "You are so funny," she said. "Where did you get your sense of humor? It's so British! The Chinese character is nearly devoid of humor."

"We try to keep it light."

"Want to go swimming?" She stripped off her clothes. "I have a bathing suit around here someplace. Even one for you."

"I've spent the last two days drugged and tied up and crated on a slow boat to China... and you stand there like that and ask if I want to swim? Well, yes... yes I do. It would take the Pacific to wash some of this crud off me. Do you have a washing machine in this place?"

"In the kitchen."

"Good. I'm in love. Bring me the swimming trunks and let me put my stuff in the washer."

"You are a patient man," she said simply.

"Another of my virtues." The trunks she tossed him were a few sizes too small.

As he emerged from the kitchen Sonya noted their fit. "Your cup of virtues runneth over," she said, opening the front door. "I'll race you to the water."

Half way to Phoenix, Beryl received a call from George. "Señor Ravenel is in jail in Buenos Aires, awaiting trial for drug smuggling. My source told me that a few months back, a real estate broker from Arizona attempted to do a background check on Señor Ravenel who was, at the time, a fugitive. The authorities played along and, once they knew where he was, they kept tabs on him and managed to take him into custody while he was, as they put it, 'in Argentine waters.' They want the story... just why we're interested in the guy. I said we'd get back to him."

"It just gets better and better," Beryl said. "Can you have the documentation about all this overnighted to Martin Mazzavini. It will be more grist for his mill. The kid is morphing into quite a sharp litigator."

As they neared Phoenix, Martin decided to call his grandfather and speak to him on the video connection. "Let's pull off the highway and get gas or something. I'm gonna call my grandfather and I'd prefer not to be distracted by traffic. I'm not gonna upset him yet with the Fed's abduction of my client from Memorial Hospital in Tucson to a Phoenix clinic. But I should touch base before we get there." Beryl moved the car into an outside lane, exited, and pulled into the parking area of a gas station.

Martin got out his phone and clicked on the video. "The first thing he'll ask me is to show him my burns," he explained.

The senior Mazzavini's secretary got the call connected to a laptop. The first words Martin could hear were curses at the complications of technology. The second words were, "I can see you, Martin. Can you see me?"

"Yes, Pop Pop. I can see you very well."

"Show me your burns."

Martin turned his face so that his grandfather could see that he still had an ear. "It's beginning to heal."

"It's all shiny. Are those blisters?"

"Yes... and the shiny stuff is the burn medication. I'm fine and I thought I'd let you know I'm on my way in to see Adam Chang."

"Not in Tucson! The feds moved him. They've got him in Phoenix... in the northwestern part... a private hospital."

Martin, on camera, could not indicate his confusion. "Yes," he said. "Yes. We're on our way there right now. You've saved his life, Pop Pop."

"I've tried to do right by him. It breaks my heart. Did I tell you that Blue Devil had head lice?"

"Yes, you did, Pop Pop. I hope they're gone by now."

"It was the dentist who saw the nits. The goddamned nits! Egg sacks still clinging to his hair. He asked Adam if his head had been shampooed with that lice soap and he said he didn't know what kind of soap it was, but evidently before you and Miss Tilson got down to the jail in Las Flores they gave him a bath and shampooed his hair to get the cooties out. I'm mad, my boy. I'm madder about this case than I've been mad about any case I can remember.

"I've gotten lab tests and copies of examinations. That boy was anemic, and he was full of vermin bites, head lice, and the x-rays of his teeth show how several had been knocked loose. They put a violent drunk into his cell! And they gave him no dental or medical assistance of any kind. They had him in limbo. The feds considered him a state prisoner and the state considered him a federal prisoner and for all their considerations they let him languish in a backwoods county jail.

"I talked to one of his professors. He's a fine boy. Tell him this Blue Devil ain't gonna let him down."

"I sure will, Pop Pop. Can you come down here for a conference on Friday?"

"For what purpose?"

"I'm calling together the principals. I want Adam brought back to Tucson and I want him to be present. And his partners, Ivan Onegin and Enrique Montoya, too. I don't know if they were part of the set-up, but they each collected two million on his partnership insurance. What their involvement was in the smuggling operation I don't know. I'm looking into it.

"Mostly I want the D.A. and the DEA people there. Adam has to be compensated. I'm gonna get the land and the distillery for him. The feds and the DA knew all along that he was innocent. They were setting up a sting of some kind and as long as he was incarcerated they thought they could operate under the radar.

"There's an operative from Hong Kong Customs, a woman by the name of Lee, who's been working with the feds on the drug trade sting. The drugs entered from Mexico near two points of entry: Sasabe and Lukeville. They were put in houses owned by the principal witnesses against Adam, Misters McPeak and Garcia - who are now dead. And then the cocaine was taken west out U.S. Highway 8, to any one of a dozen marinas where it was put on different kinds of pleasure boats or fishing boats and taken out to sea to rendezvous in international waters with a freighter bound for Hong Kong."

"I get it... the feds worry about drugs coming into the U.S. They don't pay attention to drugs going out of the U.S."

"That's about it. Mexican waters off Baja are constantly being watched, but the drugs leaving the U.S. get a free pass. Except to Hong Kong authorities."

"Where's the conference going to be held?"

"I'm gonna reserve a conference room at one of those new business-oriented motels. I think we should hold it on neutral grounds."

"Yes, good idea. Take away the "You're on my turf" atmosphere. Incidentally, the heat test results were called in to me. You were right about that gun being too hot to be held the way it was held for the camera."

"Yes, Pop Pop. I learned that the hard way. Did you get a chance to look over the Partnership Agreement?"

"Yes, and aside from Onegin and Montoya's unconscionable indifference to Mr. Chang's distress, they violated the agreement. The land and the distillery were vested in the partnership along with Adam's formulas. They said they weren't interested in mezcal production, but that was just a smokescreen so they could get their hands on the boy's intellectual property. They manipulated events until they got judgments against him that he'd never be able to satisfy. They couldn't legally touch those partnership assets for one year, yet they were showing the properties to buyers before that year was up. They even opened escrow accounts. Montoya also lied when he pledged land and said it was his. His sister owns half of it."

"Tell him about young Valentina Montoya and the trip to Nevada," Beryl said. "Ask him to get copies of all possible documents." She started the car. "I'll drive carefully while you talk."

The video call continued until a highway road sign indicated that they were two miles from the Pinnacle exit.

Martin wound down his narrative. "All right. Detainment records in Nevada, Child welfare, statutory rape, maybe the poor kid was pregnant. And see if you can find out what happened to the nun. Do you think your secretary could get copies of all of Nevada's documents regarding the arson? Anything involving Harley St. John a.k.a McPeak. And there's one other thing..."

"Name it."

"Can you get me a list of all the property that McPeak and Garcia owned in Pima County. I want it all transferred to Adam as settlement for a damages suit. McPeak and Garcia just died. Because of the drug charges, their property could be taken by federal asset-forfeiture laws. I'll need everything I can get on governmental misconduct vis-a-vis the Chang case. If they don't let the assets be turned over to Adam, I'll go to the newspapers and take the Civil Rights violations route. The feds have violated every Constitutional right Adam had and I will prove it and go public in a big way if I have to.

"And I want Montoya to compensate him by transferring title to the agave land - or I'll go public with his family's dishonorable conduct which I intend to do, anyway. And the little distillery will have to be transferred to him, too. Onegin's family is big in real estate and I'd be happy to educate the public about how they service internationally known drug dealers, the arrogant bastards.

"That Duke scholar got shafted by his partners, and by federal and state law enforcement agents. Nobody else did any suffering. An innocent genius picked up the tab for the guilty and the incompetent."

"What does that gal say, the P.I. you've been workin' with?"

Beryl laughed. "I'm encouraging him," she called out. "As it says in the Hagakure, *Continue to spur a running horse!*"

"My sentiments exactly," Mr. Mazzavini yelled. "Go for it, my boy!"

"All right, sir. I'll call you again after we speak to Adam. Oh, could you see to it that Adam's parents are brought here for the conference?"

"Consider it done. All right. I'd better get busy. Remember me to Adam."

"Will do."

Martin closed his laptop. "Ain't it nice to have helpers?" He took out his tablet and made a few cryptic notes.

When they entered Adam's room, a man was sitting beside the bed, concealing a digital recorder behind a few papers that he held in his hand.

"Who the hell are you?" Martin demanded to know.

"I'm a federal drug-enforcement agent. Stan Robinette. Who the hell are *you*?"

"Oh, me? I'm just Martin Mazzavini, Mr. Chang's attorney." Martin produced his identification. "Here's my I.D. Let me see yours." He took his quaint little blue spiral tablet out of his pocket.

As Martin copied the agent's information into his tablet, the agent grinned derisively and looked at Beryl. Martin turned on his iPhone's video reorder.

"Who's your girlfriend?" Robinette asked.

"She is my agent and is therefore legally entitled to be here. What is more important, Stan," Martin said, "is that you are *not* legally entitled to be here. I hope your job isn't contingent upon your being a licensed attorney because I'm in the mood right now to take steps to have you disbarred. You not only removed my client from Pima County's jurisdiction without notifying me, which, by the way, given his physical condition, can be construed as kidnapping; but you interrogated him and secretly recorded him and that, Stan, is a no-no. And you ransacked my room at the Arroyo Motel without benefit of a warrant. That, Stan, is a double no-no. Give me the recorder and get the hell out of here and wait in the hall until I call you. You can start acting responsibly or you can start thinking about another career. And while you wait, clear your calendar for a conference in Tucson on Friday morning. I'll tell you where and when specifically in a few hours."

Stan Robinette chuckled and put the recorder in his pocket. "I'll be out in the hall."

"The recorder, Stan." Martin extended his hand.

"The recorder stays with me."

Martin turned to Beryl. "My injuries prevent me from relieving Mr. Robinette of the illegally obtained recording of an illegal interrogation of my client. Can you help me out, here?"

Stan Robinette looked at Beryl and sneered, "Get real, Counselor." He began to walk to the door.

Beryl stepped in front of him. "I'm making a citizen's arrest," she announced, although she was not entirely sure what she meant by the remark or how making the assertion would legally protect her from putting her hands on him. Trying to maintain a serious attitude, she yelled, "You have kidnapped this young man. Stand where you are. I'm detaining you until the police arrive!" The assertion caused Agent Robinette to underestimate the threat she posed. He laughed and tried to push her out of the way. In less than two seconds he was on the floor of Adam Chang's hospital room and the digital recorder was being dropped into Beryl's tote bag.

Robinette was stunned and did not move or make a noise. Martin looked at him and then looked at Beryl. As though she were a puppy that had made a mess on the rug, Martin scolded, "Did you kill him?"

"No! Of course not." She nudged Robinette with her foot. "He's breathing."

"I'm gonna run out of patience with all these dead people!" Martin complained.

The agent groaned. Beryl reached into his holster and withdrew his gun. She extracted the magazine and checked to see that the chamber was empty.

Martin helped Robinette get to his feet. "Don't say anything, Stan. You're in deep enough shit. And you've succeeded in making my blood pressure rise. My burns are starting to hurt again. Go wait in the hall and clear your calendar for Friday in Tucson."

When the door closed behind him, Beryl asked, "How did you know it was Robinette who ransacked our rooms?"

"I didn't. But I remembered what you said about the exhumation order... just throw it out and watch people's reactions. I intended to pursue it until somebody looked guilty. He hit the first pitch."

"We have to get out of here. Stan will have a SWAT team here in about two minutes. We'll need to rent another car for you to transport Adam and the recorder back to Tucson. Adam," she said, "Put your boots on." She dropped the magazine into her tote bag and checked the closet. "Your clothes aren't here. We'll get you new stuff in Tucson."

Martin went out into the hall and saw Stan Robinette pacing back and forth, talking on his phone. He returned to the room, looked at a hospital brochure on the bedside table, and called the phone number listed. He asked for the second floor nurses' station, and then asked for Agent Robinette. As soon as the agent went to the station to answer the call, Beryl, Martin and Adam went to the rear stairwell and exited the building.

Beryl started the engine. "The hospital's security cameras will have this car on tape. They'll know what to look for on the highway. There's a car rental place up ahead. I'll meet you back at the Arroyo." She gave Martin the recorder and the magazine. "Good luck."

TUESDAY, JUNE 14, 2011

Beryl awakened at the sound of the pipes clanging as the shower was turned on in the adjoining bathroom. It was dawn. She looked at her watch on the table beside her... 6 a.m. She had been dreaming. It had been such a clear dream, but now, not thirty seconds later, she couldn't remember who was in the dream. She refused to think about anything else until she could remember. Finally one of the characters blinked into her mind. Kyle MacLachlan was discussing the film *Dune*. Maybe the desert had touched off the association.

Martin stood in the doorway with a towel wrapped around him. This time he had an announcement. "I washed our blue western shirts and jeans and even your underwear. I'm not wearing any. I hung the clothes out on the patio. I think they're dry."

"Have you ever been to a place called 'Glamis'?" she asked.

"No. I know the name... Shakespeare, isn't it? *MacBeth*?"

"Yes but that's not the Glamis I meant. There's a town south of Blythe, California, called Glamis. There are sand dunes there. It looks like the Arabian desert. They filmed many scenes from the movie *Dune* there. I could never understand the movie and I just dreamt Kyle MacLachlan was explaining it to me."

"I never understood it, either. I couldn't get past that opening backstory. Did I wake you up with the shower? I heard the pipes but it was too late to do anything about it... so I just let the cold water run. I won't be taking hot showers for months." He used a small towel to dry his hair on the left side of his head. He did not touch the right side. "Where are we going today?"

"We have questions to answer. Why did they ransack our rooms? Who slashed our tires? What happened to the $750,000 that was supposed to be drug money? What happened to the drugs that were supposed to be purchased with the drug money? Who is the reporter who tried to corrupt the jury in Adam's first trial? Who is the reporter who talked to Enrique and Steven Chang? Why didn't we know that Ivan lived in Phoenix? Who are the guys who worked with Wang Tai Tai? Who are the cigarette boat guys that intercepted Sensei and Miss Lee after the ship they were on transferred the drugs off the California coast? Have I left anything out?"

"I still can't get my mind in gear," Martin yawned. I don't know about questions. I have things to do. I just can't remember what the hell they are. Did we sleep around the clock?"

"Just about."

"When I woke up I thought about Adam. I hope he slept well in his bed in Memorial. This time hospital security isn't going to let him loose."

"It's too early to call the A.D.A. and discuss the slovenly way she's guarded the prisoner. Let's go back to sleep and find out what *Dune* is all about."

"Let's watch TV. I'll keep it low. Maybe there's a good movie on. They have porn channels that cost extra."

Beryl laughed. "If you make me laugh, you'll make me wake up. I don't want to wake up. I want to go back to sleep."

"You've already slept eleven hours. It's Tuesday."

"Shut up and watch the tube."

Beryl could not fall back to sleep. Martin put the morning news on, and she watched the show until it was time for the ADA to be in her office. Martin called and Ms. Williams told him she'd be sure to watch over her prisoner.

"She was snotty," Martin said.

"Then you should put her on your 'hit list.' She must own something you can liquify."

Martin threw a pillow at her. "Yeah," he said. "But first I'll tell her how *galactically stupid* she is."

Beryl laughed and stretched. "It's time to do what we do best. Eat."

FRIDAY, JUNE 17, 2011

It was embarrassing. Reporters and TV cameras were accosting everyone who arrived at the conference which was scheduled to begin at ten o'clock but could not get started because Sensei and Miss Lee had not yet arrived. It was ten-thirty. Adam Chang and his parents; Ivan and Enrique and their attorneys; two Mazzavinis; a secretary to the senior Mazzavini; A.D.A. Williams; DEA agent Robinette; an attorney representing the estates of McPeak and Garcia; and Beryl were all already there. But Sensei and Miss Lee were nowhere in sight.

Martin and Beryl sat at the large table, smiling weakly and apologizing every few minutes. "They said they were on their way," Martin lamely reassured the attendees. "Probably they were held up in traffic." He nervously adjusted a video projector that was pointed at a screen at the end of the conference room.

And then, at five minutes to eleven, the conference room door was flung open and Sensei and Miss Lee burst into the room, laughing. Martin nudged Beryl.

"Please have a seat," Martin said, clicking on two digital voice recorders that he placed in front of him on the table.

Martin began, "This is an impromptu meeting. None of you needs to say a word. If some of you are using digital voice recorders, you can put them on the table in front of you or you can ask ADA Loralee Williams to furnish you with a copy of this digital recording. I will give the device to her at the conclusion of the meeting. If she doesn't want it, I'll give it to the press."

Several recorders of various brands suddenly appeared on the table, standing like little sentinels in front of their owners. ADA Williams' initial expression of "confused refusal" changed into "reluctant acceptance" as she observed a few glaring looks that clearly conveyed a demand that she accept the recorder.

Martin listed and spelled the names of all who were present and gave their professional addresses.

"I'll be brief and try to speak so that all of you understand," he began, nodding to Adam Chang and his parents. "You all know what you, your agents, or your clients have done - criminally, unethically, or mistakenly - that has adversely affected my client and will require redress. I won't trouble myself to outline at this time all the various perjuries; derelictions of duty; physical abuses; breaches of partnership agreements; colluding to defraud an insurance company; withholding evidence; falsifying evidence; and a host of Constitutional rights that were violated, all to the detriment of my client. I don't want to hear that some greater good was served, that my client's freedom, reputation, and health were sacrificed to the requirements of some ongoing drug investigation. I also don't want to hear that you intended only a minor and temporary inconvenience of my client and that the continued infliction of distress was due to another agency's failure to act responsibly. This is a 'tar-baby' charge. It marks all who touch it with its guilt. In both kind and in degree, you deliberately violated the law and his rights - often in the most clownishly stupid and laughably incompetent ways. You shall be held accountable for all damage done to Adam Chang.

"There is only one way to end this scandalous misconduct without causing more innocent people to suffer ridicule, loss of honor, professional esteem, and, of course, money. That one way will be by financial compensation by the guilty parties, or by your agencies' cooperation in securing this compensation.

"Under the direction of my grandfather, Mr. Massimiliano Mazzavini, my office will prepare the various instruments of conveyance, and deliver and then receive those documents once they are executed which must be no later than June 30th, 2011. Unless all agree to all of the demands, there will be no acceptance of any; and I will be forced to make public all of the facts as I initiate actions individually against all of you. The people will then render their own judgment at trial. And if your families have to bear the shame of your dimwitted or malevolent bungling, so be it. I hasten to remind you of the suffering my client's family endured in defending him against your unconscionable actions. They lost everything that they had worked for all their lives.

"Incidentally, the reports by local hospital personnel regarding Adam Chang's physical condition when he was finally rescued from your abysmal care have been formally attested to by those who signed the reports. You will have no opportunity to alter the records."

For the next hour Martin slowly listed the instances of official misconduct. He then showed the government tape recorder and asserted that a DEA agent had attempted to persuade Adam Chang to lie under oath. Receiving a few skeptical looks, Martin paused to play a minute's worth of the tape in which Stan Robinette was unequivocally attempting to suborn perjury. Robinette squirmed in his seat and then, as his recorded voice continued to betray him, he suddenly stood up and shouted, "That is stolen government property! I want that recorder returned to me immediately!"

Martin flicked on the projector which played his iPhone's recording of Robinette's being placed under citizen's arrest and his subsequent decking. "The recording was legally obtained," Martin said. "Shut up and sit down." Fuming, Robinette sat down as everyone looked admiringly at Beryl and she smiled and nodded her appreciation.

Martin continued. He held up the laboratory reports and expert medical opinions that verified that the murder weapon could not have been handled in the way that was presented by the prosecution at trial, thereby rendering perjurious the testimonies of both Wayne McPeak and the quasi-official Hugo Garcia. He also showed reports, all dated prior to Chang's trial, from Hong Kong Customs, Interpol, and the D.E.A. that named both McPeak and Garcia as suspected drug smugglers who were targets of an ongoing investigation. These reports had been forwarded to appropriate state and federal agencies. "Allowing McPeak and Garcia to testify perjuriously against my client constitutes conspiracy in that crime." He looked at ADA Williams and shook his head and wagged his finger.

He decried the absence of a test for gunshot residue and the deplorable lack of representation. "Declaring a mistrial may have been someone's idea of a way to shed the mantle of guilt. A mistrial? Really? How vicious are you people that you would even consider putting an innocent person through that torture again. You've set a new low in bureaucratic arrogance."

As these charges hung heavily in the conference room's air, Martin proceeded to show Coast Guard Reports and Interpol memos on Gustavo Ravenel, and additional agency memos on the suspect Harley Saint John a.k.a. Harley McPeak.

Through all of Martin's recitation, Ivan Onegin and Enrique Montoya had sat impatiently, appearing to be bored, until the names of Ravenel and Harley McPeak were mentioned. The two Tres Amigos partners suddenly sat up stiffly as Martin listed their violations of the partnership agreement with Adam Chang, their "cruel indifference" to his plight - an indifference that was motivated by greed to seize his intellectual property, namely, the patent on his filtration system. Their air of immunity vaporized as Martin began to detail the sordid accounts of a family member of one partner, "an individual once regarded as a respectable real estate broker," who had colluded with the partners and with an internationally known drug dealer in an attempt to obtain land and real property that were rightfully vested in the partnership. "These machinations led to the crime of arson being committed in another state... Nevada, to be precise." Martin looked squarely at Onegin. While the room considered this never-before heard charge, Martin then turned to Beryl, *sotto voce*, and said, "How does that jingle go?" She obliged him by softly singing a few bars.

Martin then turned his gaze to Montoya. "And we shall also show how a family member of Adam Chang's other partner, who, being nefariously motivated, attempted likewise to sell this *same* parcel of land to a member of another drug smuggling operation.

"This exercise of greed and corruption was so pervasive that it numbered among its victims an innocent teenaged girl, a minor, whose misadventures with this thug resulted in her moral debauchery, her being detained by the authorities of another state, and finally, her suffering such debilitating emotional distress that she had to be hospitalized. A young nun and a friend of this girl's - neither of whom were minors at the time - were also deleteriously affected by this interstate criminal activity."

Montoya responded to these bold assertions. "You wouldn't dare! She is an innocent victim! This would destroy my father!"

Martin shrugged. "Yes, she was as innocent as Adam Chang. But I doubt that your father will lose as much as Adam's father lost. But, really, Ricky... when did you start giving a damn about anyone's innocence?"

"I require that clear title to the parcel of land upon which the murders were committed be transferred immediately to my client. I also require that title to the distillery in Nye County, Nevada, be transferred to him immediately and that the titles be equally free of any liens or encumbrances. I further require that his filtration patent be returned to him with his rights to it free and unencumbered."

Martin went on to "require" that all real property owned by Garcia and McPeak in Pima county be transferred to Adam Chang in settlement of damages and he strongly suggested that state and federal authorities re-think any attempt to invoke asset-forfeiture laws. "As a customs agent from the People's Republic of China will attest, both federal and state governments were fully aware of McPeak's and Garcia's involvement in cocaine trafficking *before* they allowed these individuals to testify against my client.

"I'm aware that in the interests of ongoing investigations, a variety of international law enforcement agencies would prefer that the facts of this case not be made public. Whether or not this entire matter is resolved quietly, without controversy, is up to all of you, collectively.

"Additionally, in regards to the shipping of this smuggled cocaine *from* American ports, Agent Sonya Lee of Hong Kong Customs, Drug Enforcement Section, will ask her superiors in Beijing *not* to make an international incident over the murders of several Chinese citizens which had recently occurred on an American vessel in U.S. waters."

Everyone looked at Sonya Lee. She did not appear to be happy. "I had been under the impression," she said slowly, "that only one week would be allowed for compliance. However, I am willing to remain in the United

States for the additional week if Mr. Mazzavini Senior will give me his assurance that he will promptly prepare, deliver, and receive the settlement documents. I can be reached through our embassy in Washington or through our consulate in San Diego. I will give each of you my card."

Massimiliano Mazzavini stood up and looked at Ms. Lee. "You have my word that I shall act promptly." He turned to his grandson and seemed officially to end the meeting. "You have been generous to the defeated, and I applaud your efforts. I confess that I would have required considerably more, but then I am an old man who has let the law creep into the marrow of his bones. What can we do with old courtroom warriors who insist on biting hard?" He looked at Miss Lee and smiled, showing the same beautiful teeth that had served him well for over sixty years.

Martin also stood up. "Thank you, Counselor. By the way, I've run out of business cards. Have you any extra on you?"

Massmiliano Mazzavini's secretary circumnavigated the large desk putting an embossed MOM card before each of the persons present.

Martin stacked the case files inside a backpack he was now using in place of an attaché case. He patted his chest to make sure his tablet was there and looked at his grandfather, "Will you be staying for dinner?"

"No," said the senior Mazzavini, "your father wants the Lear for tomorrow morning so I promised I'd get it back tonight if possible. And since you seem to have everything under control, I'll just head for the airport." He turned to the others. "It was a pleasure to have met you all."

Before he left, he kissed Mrs. Chang's hand, tweaked Beryl's nose, and bowed to Miss Lee, murmuring, "Wow."

"So who was Harley?" George asked. "Tell me again."

Beryl shrugged. "McPeak's son. There was no Mrs. McPeak. The woman he called 'his woman' - the one who fed him those pork burritos - was just an occasional girlfriend. Harley would have inherited McPeak's property but he was involved in the trafficking just as much as his father - if not more. And if Garcia had any heirs, they were in Mexico. His involvement with the drug trade would not have encouraged them to come forward."

"And the reporters?"

"I have no idea. The one who saw Mr. Chang was probably a real reporter. He'll no doubt want to write a book about this... ghost writing it with Adam, maybe."

"When is Percy getting back?"

"Ah... he's enjoying the surf in Malibu with Miss Lee. He said he is writing short Dharma talks and wonders if you'll give them for him. It's only two more weeks, George. Give the man a break. She's like a Gung Fu black belt. He's finally got a suitable playmate."

"I hate giving his Dharma talks."

"I know, George. I know."